"FREEZE, OR I'LL SHOOT IT OFF!"

Four heads whipped around. Longarm had the impression of a pretty but terribly frightened woman who stared at him. However, there wasn't time to fix anything because the would-be rapists chose to fight rather than surrender. The big man clawed for his side arm and Longarm almost enjoyed shooting him through the skull. The woman screamed as the other pair who had been holding her down also went for their guns. Longarm swung his barrel sideways and filled one of their shirt pockets with a couple of slugs.

The last man threw up his arms and bellowed, "Don't shoot!"

**DON'T MISS THESE
ALL-ACTION WESTERN SERIES
FROM THE BERKLEY PUBLISHING GROUP**

THE GUNSMITH by J. R. Roberts
Clint Adams was a legend among lawmen, outlaws, and ladies. They called him . . . the Gunsmith.

LONGARM by Tabor Evans
The popular long-running series about U.S. Deputy Marshal Long—his life, his loves, his fight for justice.

SLOCUM by Jake Logan
Today's longest-running action Western. John Slocum rides a deadly trail of hot blood and cold steel.

BUSHWHACKERS by B. J. Lanagan
An action-packed series by the creators of Longarm! The rousing adventures of the most brutal gang of cutthroats ever assembled—Quantrill's Raiders.

JOVE BOOKS, NEW YORK

LONGARM AND THE WHISKEY CREEK WIDOW

A Jove Book / published by arrangement with
the author

PRINTING HISTORY
Jove edition / April 1998

The Penguin Putnam Inc. World Wide Web site address is
http://www.penguinputnam.com

ISBN: 0-515-12265-3

A JOVE BOOK®
Jove Books are published by
The Berkley Publishing Group, a member of Penguin Putnam Inc.,
200 Madison Avenue, New York, New York 10016.
Jove and the "J" design are trademarks belonging to
Jove Publications, Inc.

PRINTED IN THE UNITED STATES OF AMERICA

10 9 8 7 6 5 4 3 2 1

LONGARM
AND THE WHISKEY
CREEK WIDOW

Chapter 1

U.S. Deputy Marshal Custis Long was about to strangle the stinking, obese gambler who'd been fouling the cramped interior of their stagecoach. Since leaving the railroad at Elko, Nevada, Longarm had been forced to endure the presence of Basil Franklin Coon for two interminable days, thanks to a broken axle and a washboard road that jarred a man's innards to jelly. But even that might have been bearable if not for Coon's incessant drinking and boastful prattle.

"And so," Coon was saying, "when I was about your age and probably in even better physical shape, I sold my cattle empire and decided to become a mine owner. I bought the Eureka Consolidated Mine on the Comstock Lode in Virginia City. Have you heard of the Comstock, Marshal Long?"

"Of course. Who hasn't?"

"Yes, of course," Coon said, taking a nip from yet another of an inexhaustible supply of pint bottles. "Anyway, some might call it luck, but I call it an astute business sense that told me that the Eureka Consolidated Mine still had a lot of ore to develop and would pay off handsomely."

"And it did," Longarm commented, wanting to reach the end of this latest boastful lie in a hurry.

"You bet it did!" Coon exclaimed. "Why, I became as rich as a king! I kept crews working that hardrock mine day and night for two years, and we sent about three million dollars worth of gold and silver over to the smelter just outside of Carson City. I tell you, I had quite an operation and . . ."

Coon stopped. "I probably shouldn't brag about this, but . . ."

"Why stop now?" Longarm said cryptically. "Brag on."

"Ha!" Coon cried, slapping his fat thigh. "That's what I like best about you, Marshal, you've a great sense of humor."

"I'm glad that you think so."

"Want a little nip?"

"No, thanks."

"Then I'll have yours! Ha!"

Longarm sighed and gazed forlornly out the window as Coon droned on and on about how he'd made, and then given away, a fortune. Despite his exasperation, Longarm had to admit that Coon was at least a very creative bullshitter. Longarm tried to ignore the man and study the surroundings.

This part of eastern Nevada was pretty country, and the distant Ruby Mountains were green and still snowcapped although it was June. However, down at this lower elevation, the desert was warm and the road plenty dusty. Longarm wondered how long it would take to track down the three men who had robbed the Elko National Bank. They had shot the bank manager and then cold-bloodedly executed the three others who could have testified as witnesses. Had it not been for a couple of sharp-eyed citizens directly across the street, the three bank robbers might actually have escaped unseen. Whiskey Creek was now Longarm's immediate destination because that was the place where the three bank robbers had last been spotted.

The trouble was that the stagecoach agent hadn't warned Longarm that the only other passenger on this run would be Basil Franklin Coon, or that the damned coach would strand them an extra day while a broken axle was fixed.

"I believe that you said you worked out of the government office in Denver," Coon was saying. "Does my memory serve me well?"

"It does."

"Well," Coon said heavily, "I'm sure that you've never really had any money. Lawmen are always underpaid."

"That's the truth." Longarm stuck his head out the window, gulping clean, high-desert air and wondering if Basil Coon had ever bathed.

"A man like you ought to consider working for himself instead of always having to suck up to a boss. Marshal Long, you look like a bright, enterprising man."

"Thanks."

"So," Coon said, picking his teeth with a dirty thumbnail, "why don't you go off on your own instead of continuing to suck the government's tit?"

Longarm ground his teeth and tried to keep from losing his temper. Nothing would be gained by insulting this boor because Coon was too insensitive and self-absorbed to even realize that he was being maligned. Violence was also out of the question because Longarm didn't want to bring any shame on himself or his office by assaulting the obnoxious fool. As a lawman, Custis was sworn to protect, not dismantle, public citizens. If Longarm's patience snapped and he accidently broke Coon's piggish little nose, word might get back to Denver and that would reflect badly on Longarm's reputation.

Coon eyed Longarm with skepticism. "Tell me one thing, Marshal Long. Have you ever done anything else except work for the government?"

"Yeah," Longarm said through clenched teeth, "I've done quite a few things."

"Such as?"

"Such as mind my own business."

"Hmmm, well, that's nice," Coon said, looking disgusted rather than impressed. "But it won't get you rich. And when I say 'rich,' I mean rich enough to do whatever you want when you want. Do you understand me, Marshal?"

"I understand you," Longarm said, wondering how much longer it would take to reach Whiskey Creek. According to the driver, they should already have been in sight of the damned mining town.

"Do you have any investment money?" Coon asked.

Longarm hadn't been listening. "What?"

"Investment money," Coon repeated. "You know, some capital to either start a business or buy one."

"No."

Coon shook his head so hard that his great, sagging jowls wagged. "I was very much afraid of that. Without investment capital, a man is at the mercy of every two-bit employer in America."

"I work for the federal government."

"No matter. The government is even worse than most private companies and it pays nothing. Listen, Marshal, if you have anything of value that you could hand over to me as security—such as that fine gold watch and chain—I'd be willing to loan you some start-up capital. Perhaps up to a hundred dollars . . . at ten-percent interest."

"No, thanks."

"I wouldn't mind. You being a federal officer, I know that, while you don't get paid much, at least you get paid regular. Only thing is, you might get shot in the line of duty and then I'd lose my money. That's why I'd have to charge you ten percent . . . a month."

Longarm blinked. He was a big man, six feet four inches, with a broad, handsome face, steel-blue eyes, and a mustache darker than the dust that coated his tanned face. Because of the bouncing coach and the tight confines, Longarm had removed his snuff-brown Stetson and brown suit coat. His vest revealed a blue-gray shirt, and his string tie was stuffed into his pocket.

"I don't want a loan and I like my job fine, Basil. So drop the subject, all right?"

"Sure," the fat man said, throwing up his hands but looking as if his feelings were injured. "You want to stay poor, that's your choice."

"Exactly."

"What time you got, Marshal?"

Longarm reached into his vest and removed his Ingersol 1 watch, which was connected by a gold chain to a .44-caliber derringer lying hidden in his other vest pocket. "Five minutes after two."

"We should have arrived in Whiskey Creek by now," Coon complained.

"We should have been there yesterday afternoon!"

"That's right, and it is the stagecoach company's fault that this damned coach broke an axle. I am going to demand a full refund plus a fee for my time and inconvenience when we arrive in Whiskey Creek. I suggest that you and I find the agent and also seek immediate compensation."

"You can't predict a busted axle," Longarm pointed out.

"That's not the point. They should equip these coaches with heavier axles. I'm telling you that we have suffered damages and I will not be satisfied until we collect!"

"This is a good stage line, Basil. The busted axle was just bad luck."

Coon stared at him in amazement. "Are you telling me that you'll refuse to ask for just compensation?"

"That's right," Longarm snapped with annoyance. "Out here, things like this happen all the time. People just do the best that they can with what they got. There are no guarantees about anything. I suggest that you accept that fact of Western life and just do whatever you mean to do in Whiskey Creek.''

''What I mean to do is buy another mine!'' Coon leaned forward, his foul breath washing over Longarm like sewer water. ''Would you be interested in a partnership? I would be willing to issue you a few shares for that fine pocket watch and chain.''

''Not interested.''

''But I can guarantee that you will double your money within a month! So, in addition to the watch, how much money can you invest?''

''Nothing. Not one damned dollar.''

Coon leaned back as if slapped. ''Marshal, perhaps you simply don't understand the kind of opportunity that I'm offering you. This is your chance to become rich, or at least comfortable. I know that you have no business acumen, but I will gladly advise you and make you a lot of money.''

''What money I have, I need.''

''Oh, yes, I forgot,'' Coon said cryptically as he leaned back on his bench seat. ''You're on the trail of those three Elko bank robbers. Well, if I were you, I'd just forget about them and give me the money to invest. After you've doubled your investment, you can pocket your profits and then go after that trio of murderers.''

''I don't work that way, Basil.''

Coon's voice took on a note of desperation. ''Marshal, don't throw away the chance of a lifetime!''

''Sorry.''

Coon took a long drink, and his voice reeked with disgust when he said, ''I see now that I overestimated you, Marshal. The problem is that you have no guts.''

''No what?'' Longarm asked, not believing his ears.

''No guts,'' Basil Coon repeated, lifting his bottle again to his porcine little lips. ''You don't have the courage to invest, and so you'll never have any money. You are, from an investment standpoint, simply a coward.''

Longarm's fist drove the bottle halfway down Basil Franklin Coon's flabby throat. The man's eyes bugged and his throat worked as terror corroded his features. Coon tried to extract the bottle, his fingers desperately trying to work it back out of his mouth as his complexion turned bright red.

"Why don't you swallow it," Longarm said, folding his arms across his chest. "Or better yet, just suck on it a while and give me some peace."

Coon's eyes bugged even more, and his nostrils flared. Longarm watched with interest, but when the man's face begin to turn blue, he became a little concerned.

"What's the matter?" Longarm asked. "Pull the damned thing out!"

But Basil Coon's eyes were starting to roll upward. Longarm leaned forward, suddenly alarmed. "Come on, Basil, spit the damned bottle out!"

Coon's pudgy hands fluttered helplessly, and then he pitched forward, making awful choking sounds.

"Oh, kee-rist!" Longarm swore in alarm. "He's going to choke to death!"

Longarm didn't want to do it, but he tried to pull the end of the bottle out of Coon's mouth. When that didn't work, he balled his fist and began to whack Coon between his meaty shoulders. He hit the man so hard that Coon's entire body shook until the whiskey bottle finally popped free.

Basil Coon lay wedged between the seats, whooping for air and making horrible sounds as he tried to fill his tortured lungs. Longarm, thoroughly disgusted, opened the door and then climbed up on the roof, breathing in the clean perfume of desert sage.

The stagecoach driver looked at him with a question, prompting Longarm to say, "I needed some fresh air!"

"Yes, sir, Marshal! The wonder is that you put up with that blowhard as long as you did. I thought you'd be up here a whole lot sooner."

"My mistake," Longarm said, feeling much better. "Say, are those mustangs out there on that plateau?"

"You bet they are! There's more mustangs in this part of Nevada than anyplace I've ever seen."

Longarm admired a blood-red stallion and his band of about six mares. There were several yearlings as well and they stood stiff and alert, watching the stagecoach pass at a quarter-mile distance.

"Them mustangs won't be here much longer," the driver said, looking upset.

"Why not?"

"They're being killed off for their hides and tails."

Longarm did not understand. He knew that mustangs were often hunted and broken for saddle horses, and some were sent East to be slaughtered, but skinned and their tails lopped off?

"Why?"

"The Orientals want the tails and pay top dollar for 'em," the driver explained with a shrug of his shoulders. "Beats me what they want 'em for, but they want 'em, and the tails of the foals are supposed to be the most valuable."

"What a shame!"

"Yeah," the driver said. "The hides are shipped back East. Altogether, a dead mustang is worth about ten dollars, and that's why they're being hunted and slaughtered by the thousands."

This was troubling news to Longarm. And although he did not own a horse and most of his travel was by rail and coach, he enjoyed horses and thought them the most beautiful of God's creatures, next to a woman.

"Yep," the driver was saying, "the mustang killers ride out here with high-powered buffalo rifles and shoot 'em, or else they trap the whole band. There used to be a lot more mustangs hereabouts."

"I don't approve one damned bit," Longarm said angrily.

"The ranchers in this country sure do, though," the driver said. "They hate mustangs because, in poor years when the grass doesn't grow high, their cattle go hungry. To a cattle rancher, the mustang is just a competitor that needs to be eliminated. He views 'em about the same as he views a coyote."

"Too bad," Longarm said with a shake of his head as they drove the last few miles into Whiskey Creek.

Chapter 2

The stagecoach driver named Andy glanced sideways at Longarm and drawled, "Marshal Long?"

"Yeah?"

"You strike me as a tough, sensible fella. Mind if I give you a little piece of advice?"

"Nope."

"If I were you," Andy said, "I'd hide that silver star you're wearing before we pull into Whiskey Creek. The town has a reputation for killing lawmen."

Longarm reached into his pocket and extracted the stub of a five-cent cheroot. "Is that a fact?"

"It is, Marshal. This town is lawless. It's every man, woman, and child for themselves."

"Sounds pretty rough."

"Whiskey Creek is *worse* than bad." The grizzled old veteran driver with a face like rawhide spat a stream of tobacco over the side of the coach. "The thing of it is, Marshal, the miners get drunk every night and raise hell. There are a few wealthy saloon owners who pretty much pull the strings, and you can't walk the street without taking a chance of gettin' shot by some drunken, trigger-happy sonofabitch."

"And there's no law?"

''Nope. They've all been gunned down or tarred, feathered, and run out of town.''

They were still about a quarter mile from the town, but Longarm could see that Whiskey Creek was a fairly substantial collection of buildings. It was situated at the base of a pine-and-pinyon-covered mountain, and there was a road leading up into a canyon that was in heavy use. Longarm had seen a lot of frontier towns, many of them mining rather than ranching communities. He estimated that this one would have about three thousand citizens, more than enough to hire a sheriff and build a jail, a church, and a schoolhouse.

''Are the mines located in that canyon just beyond the town itself?'' Longarm asked.

''Yep. Whiskey Creek was founded about six years ago when a pair of brothers struck it rich up in that rocky canyon. Inside a month, there were four or five thousand prospectors crawling all over these hills. But in the last few years, gold and silver production has been falling and the town is slowly dying. I guess that's why the miners drink so hard.''

''They'll usually manage to find an excuse if that's what they're of a mind to do,'' was Longarm's comment. ''Besides, there's always the chance that another vein of gold will be discovered.''

''There's that,'' the stagecoach driver agreed. ''In fact, before we left Elko, our smelly passenger friend tried to get me to hand over some of my earnings and become a partner in what he figured would be Whiskey Creek's next big strike.''

''Yeah.'' Longarm chuckled. ''Mr. Coon would have settled for my watch and gold chain. I have the feeling that our traveling companion is a little short of funds.''

''Probably used 'em to buy all those pint bottles of whiskey,'' the driver said. ''I about busted my gut trying to lift that big satchel of 'em into the boot before we left Elko.''

"Well," Longarm said consolingly, "I can assure you that the satchel will be considerably lighter when we come to a rest in Whiskey Creek."

"Sure sorry about the delay we had over that broken axle, Marshal Long. I can imagine what a sonofabitchin' time you've had ridin' down there in the company of that braggin' bastard."

Longarm just shook his head. "I travel so much that I meet all kinds. And I have a feeling that Mr. Coon is going to be rather quiet for the next few days while his throat heals."

The driver shot a questioning glance at Longarm. "You shoved your fist down his throat?"

"No, a bottle."

Andy threw his head back and laughed all the rest of the way into Whiskey Creek.

As they rolled into the mining settlement, Longarm could see that this was indeed a wild and lawless town. It was only mid-afternoon, but already there were dozens of miners staggering from one saloon to another. Longarm saw no less than five men passed out drunk in the street. The front windows of most of the stores had been boarded over, and whiskey and beer bottles were scattered everywhere.

A fight that originated inside the Hard Luck Bar swirled out into the street blocking the stagecoach's path.

"Whoa!" Andy yelled, pulling up sharply on the lines as the combatants rolled, kicked, punched, and gouged in the dirt. There were eight men fighting and it was a donnybrook. Longarm considered breaking up the fight, but decided to hell with it. That was a good way to get yourself hurt for no good reason, and besides, these men weren't using guns or knives. They were just bludgeoning each other senseless with their fists.

Dozens of miners surged out on the town's boardwalk to cheer their favorites. Unhappy with the way things were going, scores of the spectators joined the fight and within a few moments, more than a hundred men were beating the hell out of each other. It looked to Longarm as if there was a full-scale riot taking place on the main street.

Andy hauled his stagecoach up short and announced, "I'm going to back up this coach and go around to a side street in order to get us to the stage yard. I sure as hell don't want us caught in the middle of this."

Longarm grabbed his traveling bag and rifle. "Andy, I'm getting off right here."

"I sure wish you'd take my advice and put that star in your pocket," Andy said with a shake of his head. "You're a nice fella and I'd just as soon not see you bushwhacked."

"Is that what happened to the last marshal?"

"Yep. And the one before him."

"Miners have a reputation for getting drunk and fighting," Longarm said, "but I never thought of them as ambushers or backshooters."

"It may not be the miners that are doing the shooting," Andy said. "I figure it's the saloon owners that want this town wide open and without any law except their own."

Longarm didn't have anything to say about that. As a federal marshal, it really was not his job to meddle with local issues. He'd been heading back to the Federal Building in Denver when his boss, Marshal Billy Vail, intercepted him with a telegram ordering him to catch the next train west to Elko and start after the three bank robbers. Longarm hadn't been too happy about the sudden turnaround, but orders were orders, and that was why he preferred not to get sidetracked with the lawlessness here in Whiskey Creek.

"Good luck!" Andy called as Longarm swung down from the top of the stage and headed toward the nearest hotel.

"Wait!" a voice cried. "Marshal Long, please, wait up!"

Longarm paused, then turned to see Basil Coon tumble headfirst out of the coach and land heavily in the street. During the moment that Coon lay helpless and stunned, two unsavory-looking fellows jumped off the boardwalk and ran over to fleece his pockets.

Longarm couldn't stomach Coon, but he wasn't about to stand by and allow the braggart to be robbed either. "Hey!" he shouted, waving his rifle. "Get away from that man!"

The pair of thieves were in the act of stooping over poor Coon when Longarm's sharp warning straightened them in their tracks. They took one look at Longarm and the badge on his coat and decided that they wanted no part of the federal marshal. However, in pure spite, one of the men booted Coon in the ribs. The fat man cried out in pain, then lost consciousness.

Longarm could have either shot the thieves or run them down, but his immediate concern was Basil Coon. He glanced up at the stagecoach driver. "Do you want to give me a hand and drag his carcass into the hotel?"

"Sorry," Andy yelled. "But if I left this stage even for one minute, someone would steal everything they could pry loose off of it. Hope you understand, Marshal. I could lose my job if I allowed that to happen. Best thing to do is just leave that fat braggart."

"I can't do that in good conscience. Mister!" Longarm yelled at a huge bearded miner who looked to be sober. "Do you want to earn a dollar?"

"Sure!"

"Then carry this man into that hotel lobby."

The miner stepped forward, rolling his heavy shoulders and wiping his dirty hands on his shirtfront. He was a redheaded giant, but when he grabbed Basil Coon and tried to pick him up, he couldn't begin to do the job. "Too damned heavy for me," the giant said, placing his hand against the small of his back and wincing.

"All right," Longarm said, knowing something had to be done for Coon, "then just drag him into the lobby."

"Now, I can do that," the giant said, grabbing Coon's ankles and jerking him forward. "My Lord, this fella must weigh close to four hundred pounds!"

"For sure," Longarm said.

"Whew!" the giant exclaimed, wrinkling his nose. "Has your friend got something against soap and water?"

"I guess," Longarm conceded, "although he sure likes whiskey."

"Nothing wrong with that, but he ought to take a bath every year or two."

"I couldn't agree with you more." Longarm shifted his rifle across his arm. "Let's go."

It was all the giant could do to drag the unconscious Basil Coon into the hotel. The miner stopped and grunted and was sweating like a horse after only dragging the fat man thirty yards and then rolling him onto the boardwalk. Then, with his strength visibly flagging, he dragged Basil the last few feet into the hotel.

"Is that far enough, Marshal? My back is killin' me."

"No."

"Aw, come on," the giant protested. "My back is worth more than a damn dollar!"

"All right," Longarm said, "just drag him over beside the couch and I'll pay you."

The giant grunted some more, and when he was finished and had been paid, he complained bitterly. "That sure wasn't worth the dollar, Marshal. That there is the fattest, smelliest man I ever seen. You got a real poor choice of friends."

"Just get out of here," Longarm said, moving over to the registration desk where a wolf-faced man in his sixties stood wearing a scowl.

"I need a room."

"A dollar a day—in advance," the man said. "You get

a bucket of water and, the last I seen, my outhouse don't have no black widder spiders hidin' under the toilet seat.''

''Great,'' Longarm said.

The hotelman raised a bony finger and pointed at Basil Coon. ''What about that one?''

''I don't know,'' Longarm said, going back to the still-unconscious man. ''I suggest that you wait and ask him what he wants to do when he wakes.''

The hotelman made an unpleasant face as if he'd bitten into a lemon before he turned back to Longarm. ''How many nights you want to pay for in advance, Marshal?''

''From what I hear, my life expectancy is pretty low in Whiskey Creek. That being the case, I think that I'll just pay you for one night at a time.''

''You better get shot somewhere's else,'' the man warned. ''I don't want no killin' in my place.''

''I'll keep that in mind,'' Longarm said cryptically as he paid for his first night's lodging. ''By the way, have you seen three strangers who rode into Whiskey Creek and began to spend a lot of money?''

''No.''

''Think hard. These are rough-looking fellas. One has a long scar down the right side of his face. Another has part of his left ear bitten off, and the third, from what I'm told, wears a pearl-handled Colt on his left hip and uses a cross draw just the same as I do.''

''Never heard nor seen 'em,'' the hotelman said, pinning his eyes on Longarm's federal marshal's badge. ''And even if I had, I wouldn't tell. I don't like lawmen and I never have.''

''That figures,'' Longarm said in a cold voice. ''You look the type that would rob his own mother for a dollar.''

The man paled slightly before he drew back his lips to reveal bad teeth as he hissed, ''Marshal, if I were a betting man, I'd bet that you'll be sleepin' in our cemetery tonight.''

"Give me my room key."

It was Room 4, and Longarm had no trouble finding it because there were only ten rooms altogether. The room was spartan, but at least it was clean and it had fresh linen and a blanket. Longarm didn't suppose that the hotel would offer the services of a bath, so he used a porcelain pitcher and washbasin to clean himself up. He changed his shirt and shaved, then dusted off his Stetson, and headed out to the lobby for the front door after making sure that his Colt revolver was in good working order.

"Marshal!"

Longarm didn't want to stop but the cry was so plaintive, he came to a standstill, turned, and said, "What the hell is it now, Basil?"

"I've been robbed! That man behind the desk emptied my pockets!"

"I did not!" the hotel clerk shouted. "I wouldn't get near ya, ya overstuffed pig!"

Basil came to his feet. He was still groggy, but there was no doubt that he intended to grab and strangle the much smaller man. Longarm intercepted Basil Coon, and it was like stopping a small freight train. "Hold up there, Basil! How much money is missing?"

Coon pushed Longarm back about four more feet, and glared at the hotel clerk. "Marshal Long, I swear to you that I had six dollars and change."

"All right then," Longarm said, "you can have six nights free lodging in this hotel."

"The hell you say!" the hotel clerk shouted.

Longarm spun around on his heel and marched over to the desk. He leaned across it and warned, "If you open your trap once more, I will personally rearrange those rotting teeth. Is that understood?"

The man nodded fearfully.

"Good!" Longarm wheeled around. "Basil, you get a room and you find a bath!"

"But I'm without funds!"

Longarm stopped at the door, reached into his pocket, and found a silver dollar. "You use that on a bath."

"Marshal, I'm hungry!"

"Damn!" Longarm found a second dollar. "A meal and then a bath. But that's it! Afterward, find a way to buy yourself a gold mine and get rich, hear me?"

Coon nodded vigorously.

Satisfied, Longarm marched outside and up the street, not really sure of where he was going next. It was his custom to always pay a courtesy call on the local authorities to announce his presence. Often, that meant a pleasant visit with the town marshal in which they would sometimes swap war stories about their most hair-raising experiences with outlaws. But now, since there was no local authority to visit and to ask about the three Elko bank robbers, Longarm was a little unsure of where he should begin.

It was possible, of course, that he might be able to stumble across the three outlaws and simply make his arrest. Possible, but not very likely. However, it was worth a try, so Longarm decided that he would begin his hunt and that, perhaps, it would be wisest to take the stagecoach driver's advice and slip his badge into his coat pocket. After all, what was the point in creating any more problems?

The big fight in the street had broken up, but some of the combatants were pretty battered and still down. Longarm shook his head with disapproval and went into the Wildcat Waterhole, a very unsavory-looking drinking establishment. It was not large, about twenty by twenty feet, and the bar itself was nothing but a wooden plank resting across two empty whiskey kegs.

"What will you have, stranger?" the bartender asked.

"A beer."

"My beer is green and my whiskey is too," the bartender explained, "but at least the whiskey is strong enough to kill whatever breeds and swims in it."

"In that case, I'll take the whiskey."

The bartender produced a bottle and a chipped glass. "Stranger, are you lookin' for work?" he asked, sizing Longarm up and seeming to approve. "You strike me as a man that can use a gun."

"I'm not looking for work," Longarm said. "I'm looking for some old friends that I heard were recently in town. Maybe you can help me find them."

"Maybe," the bartender said without enthusiasm, "for a price."

Longarm described the trio while the bartender helped himself to a drink from Longarm's bottle at his customer's expense. When Longarm was finished with his description, he said, "That's about all I can tell you."

"No names?" the bartender asked. "What kind of friends are these that have no names?"

"They're the kind that change their names depending on the circumstances," Longarm explained with a wink. "I'm sure that you've known that type."

The bartender leaned forward. "How much is information worth to you?"

"How much information have you to sell?"

"About five dollars' worth."

Longarm reached into his pocket and found the money. Laying it on the bar, he placed his hand over the greenbacks and said in a low voice, "Now, you tell me what you know and I'll decide what it's worth."

"Fair enough. The men you are searching for arrived in Whiskey Creek, but they didn't stay more than a few days. As a matter of fact, I remember them riding out of town about two days ago."

"Going where?"

The bartender shrugged, his fingers inching closer to the bills that Longarm still protected. "Beats me."

"What direction were they riding?"

"South, but they could have changed directions the moment they left town and I'd have no way of knowing.''

The bartender lowered his voice to make sure that he could not be overheard by some of the customers down the bar. ''To be honest, those three spent some time in this saloon and they were real hardcases. They claimed they were looking for work in the mines, but I knew they were lying.''

''How?''

''They were gunmen, not miners. They wore their pistols sort of like you do. You know what I mean?''

''Not exactly.''

''All right,'' the bartender said, leaning forward on his elbows. ''They wore their guns like they were part of their bodies. Like they used them a lot. The miners wear guns, but mostly they just stuff them into their waistbands. You can tell that they'd rather beat each other half to death in a good old-fashioned fistfight instead of shoot each other. The men you are hunting would shoot first and enjoy killing.''

''I see. Can you tell me where they were staying?''

''Down at The Hotel. That's what it's called, The Hotel. It's the best in Whiskey Creek and these three friends of yours had plenty of money. They drank hard and they liked to play cards.''

''Were they any good?''

''No.'' The bartender chuckled. ''My boys lightened their wallets considerably. They would have gotten even more of their money except that the three would get real dangerous after losing a few hundred dollars. I told my players just to take what they could but not to get so greedy that bullets started flying.''

Longarm lifted his hand off the bills. The information was worth five dollars, but it was quite disappointing. It meant that he would have to rent or buy a horse and take up the outlaws' trail to God knows where.

''I guess I'm going to need a good horse,'' Longarm

said, unable to hide his discouragement. "Who shall I talk to?"

"I can fix you up with a horse, saddle, and outfit."

"But you're a bartender."

"I'm a *businessman.*"

"All right," Longarm said. "I'll take a look at what you have to offer."

The bartender dug into his apron and found a pencil and pad of paper. He scribbled a note and then signed his own name: Pete. "Here," he said, handing Longarm the note. "You take this down to the Flatrock Livery and ask for Duncan."

"Duncan?"

"That's right. He's a crusty old fart, but he owes me a favor and he'll treat you right."

"He'd better," Longarm said. "I do know horses and I won't buy one that will go lame."

"Horses are cheap in this part of the country if you don't mind buying a Nevada mustang."

"I'd rather not."

"You'll change your mind when you see the quality of mustangs that Duncan has to offer. He's real picky about his horses and has some damned fine ones."

"Most of 'em are much too small to pack a man of my size very far," Longarm explained.

But the bartender shook his head. "He's got some mustangs that'll weight a thousand pounds and will run for miles without getting winded. Trust me. You'll like the horses and you'll like Duncan's prices."

"And what do you get out of this?"

Pete smiled. "I'd like you to buy me this bottle of green whiskey."

"Which costs?"

"Five more dollars."

Longarm frowned. "All right," he finally said, "but if

Duncan and I can't come to terms, I'll be back for that second five dollars.''

''Duncan will come to terms and you won't regret using my services,'' Pete promised. ''When you get outside, turn right and keep walking. The Flatrock Livery is at the end of town. You'll see about four pens of mustangs and some of them have actually been ridden.''

Longarm headed for the door just shaking his head.

Chapter 3

Longarm was striding along the boardwalk, minding his own business, when he heard a cry for help. It was a muffled cry, and it brought Longarm up short in his tracks because it sounded like a woman's voice. Taking a few more steps forward, he glanced to his right between a pair of dilapidated buildings into a corridor of dark shadow. For a moment, Longarm saw nothing. Then he heard the cry again.

"Please, no!"

Longarm reached across his waist, drew his Colt .44 revolver, and hurried down between the buildings. He could hear a young woman whimpering in addition to the rough and coarse grunting of men. As Longarm neared the end of the buildings, he could see that he was about to enter an alley. Taking a deep breath, Longarm stepped around the corner and raised his six-gun.

A young, dark-haired woman was on her back and her skirts were shoved up around her waist as two men held her and a third was about to mount her. The men were so excited that they didn't even hear Longarm's hammer cock or see him step closer.

The largest of the three was kneeling between the woman's legs. He had his tool in his fist and he was leering down at his intended victim when Longarm yelled, "Freeze or I'll shoot it off!"

Four heads whipped around. Longarm had the impression of a pretty but terribly frightened woman who stared at him. However, there wasn't time to fix anything because the would-be rapists chose to fight rather than surrender. The big man clawed for his side arm, and Longarm almost enjoyed shooting him through the skull. The woman screamed as the other two who had been holding her down also went for their guns. Longarm swung his barrel sideways and filled one of their shirt pockets with a couple of slugs.

The last man threw up his hands and bellowed, "Don't shoot!"

Longarm wanted to shoot. He really did, but it would have been murder so he held his fire. At the same time, the woman tugged her skirts down, climbed unsteadily to her feet, and ran over to throw herself into Longarm's embrace. She was sobbing and hugging Longarm's neck so tightly that he had trouble breathing and his line of fire was blocked.

"Let loose of me!" Longarm shouted, pushing her aside as the last man turned and ran for his life.

Longarm raised his pistol and took aim on the would-be rapist. "Stop, I'm a United States deputy marshal and I'll shoot!"

But the man did not stop, so Longarm had no choice but to put a couple of slugs into the backs of his flying legs. The man howled with pain and his legs broke at the knees. He spilled to the ground and started dragging himself away.

"Miss," Longarm said, struggling to extract himself from her viselike embrace, "I have to get that man. Would you please let go of me?"

She gathered her composure and stepped away, but not before the wounded man had almost rounded a building.

He might have escaped if Longarm had not broken free and sprinted to overtake him.

"That's about far enough," Longarm said, pressing the muzzle of his Colt against the back of the attacker's skull.

The man froze, then slowly turned to look up at Longarm. "Marshal, I wasn't going to do it to her!"

"Not first, maybe, but for sure second or third," Longarm growled.

Tears filled the wounded man's eyes. "I'm shot real bad in the legs. I think I'm bleeding to death!"

"That would be a blessing for humanity. If I wasn't sworn to uphold the law, I'd save the hangman the bother of finishing you off."

"But she's a breed!" the man cried. "Half Indian! I swear it."

Longarm was filled with loathing and disgust. It was all that he could do not to put another bullet through both the man's kneecaps and watch him die in agony.

"I need a doctor!"

A shaky voice behind Longarm said, "If you can't shoot him, then give your damned gun to me and I'll do it."

Longarm turned to study the young woman. He could see now that she really was part Indian, with her raven's-wing black hair parted in the center and her dark eyes. She wore a turquoise necklace with matching earrings, and even though she was in disarray, she was obviously quite a beauty.

"I can't let you shoot him either," Longarm said. "It would be murder. I will, however, promise you that justice will be served."

She met his eyes. "How? My husband was the marshal of this town and he's dead. Who is going to arrest and watch over this man while he is a prisoner?"

"I will," Longarm said. "I'll make sure that he is jailed until a judge can sentence him."

"You'll take my husband's place?"

"Only for the few days that might be necessary, and then I have to leave and run down some outlaws." Longarm knelt beside the wounded man. "Does this town have a doctor?"

"No," she said.

"But it does have a jail?"

"Of course."

Longarm heaved a deep sigh. "Then let's get him to the jail and I'll see if I can dig the bullets out of his legs."

The wounded man's eyes widened with horror. "No!"

"Suit yourself," Longarm said, standing erect. "Either the bullets come out or you'll probably die of blood poisoning or gangrene."

The wounded man clenched his teeth, obviously in great pain. "For gawd sakes, I need whiskey! Something . . . anything . . . to kill the pain."

"If the marshal will give me his gun, I'll be happy to put you out of your pain," the young woman offered, her black eyes blazing with hatred.

"Go to Hell!"

The woman shook with fury and, for a moment, Longarm thought she was going to attack. Instead, she turned and started back up the alley.

"Hey!" Longarm shouted. "If this man is going to stand before a judge, I'll need you to testify!"

"No!" she called.

Longarm swore in anger. "What's your name?"

But the woman didn't answer. Longarm looked down at the wounded man. "What's her name?"

"Donita. Donita York. She's nothing."

"The hell you say," Longarm grated, extending his hand. "Come on, get up!"

"I can't stand!"

"Sure you can," Longarm said, hauling the man to his feet and ignoring his pitiful sobbing. "You're going to walk or I'm going to leave you here to bleed to death. Which is it going to be?''

The man cursed, but he allowed Longarm to help him move forward. ''Just point us to the jail and let's hope you don't bleed to death before we get there,'' Longarm said, not much caring if the man died or not.

The jail wasn't much. Just a stone rectangle of about three hundred square feet. A grate of iron bars extended across the back of the jail, and the front part was crowded with a desk and chairs, along with a workbench with a half-finished saddle and several bridles and harnesses in various stages of repair. It was clear that the town marshal had been a saddle maker and leather worker in order to supplement his meager salary.

By the time Longarm had his prisoner in the jail, the man was as pale as a ghost and too weak to stand. ''I'm gonna die,'' he whimpered. ''You shot three white men over a breed, you crazy bastard.''

''You deserve to die,'' Longarm said, utterly without sympathy. ''Halfbreed, full Indian, it doesn't matter. Where I come from, a man doesn't act like an animal around women, even the bad ones.''

''Where the hell do you come from!''

''West-by-God-Virginia,'' Longarm said, removing his pocketknife and cutting the man's pants legs up to his thighs so that he could examine the gunshot wounds.

One of his bullets had passed through the man's calf muscle, and while it was probably very painful, the bullet had not severed any big arteries, nor had it shattered the leg bone.

''Your right lower leg might feel as if it is blown off,'' Longarm announced, ''but it's just a flesh wound.''

''Good. What about the left?''

Longarm conducted a very quick examination. ''It's in bad shape,'' he said without preamble. ''My bullet hit you in the knee and shattered the hell out of it."

"I'll never walk right again!"

"That's about the size of it," Longarm agreed. "But it would help if I could dig out the lead so the knee would at least heal."

The man wiped sweat from his brow with the back of his sleeve. "You ever did this kind of thing before, Marshal?"

"About fifty times."

"And they all lived?"

"I didn't say that."

"Then for gawdsake don't cut on me!"

"Fine," Longarm said as he started to leave the cell. "You can just lie here and rot for all I care."

"Wait!"

Longarm paused. Despite his disgust for this man, he could not help but feel a little pity. "What's it going to be?"

"You got a sharp knife?"

"Yes."

The man swallowed. "Marshal, will you at least buy me a bottle of whiskey to drink first?"

"Do you have the money?"

"I do."

"All right," Longarm agreed, going back into the cell. "I'll buy a bottle. Give me the money."

The man reached for his inside coat pocket and, if Longarm had not been a man of considerable experience, he would have been caught flat-footed by the deception. Instead of money, out came a single-shot .45-caliber derringer, the kind that was very popular with gamblers and back-alley murderers. Longarm's hand battled the ugly little weapon aside and it fired, tearing a hole in the beamed ceiling.

Balling up his fist, Longarm smashed the man in the face, not once, but twice.

"There," Longarm said to his unconscious prisoner, "I guess you're going to get through this surgery with a lot less pain than either one of us figured. But you're going to have a shiner and a dislocated jaw."

Longarm didn't waste any time with preliminaries. He'd removed bullets not only from men he'd shot and ridden with, but also from his own scarred body. Wiping his pocketknife on his pants leg, he made a quick and deep incision, then jammed his thumb and forefinger into the wound, exploring it for the misshapen lead and the fragments of shattered bone that he knew he'd find.

It was bloody but fast work. In less than a quarter of an hour, Longarm had removed all the lead and the bone that he could feel or see. There would be small pieces of both still inside the knee, but removing them was beyond his skill or patience.

"If you don't get sentenced and hanged," he told his unconscious patient, "you're going to walk with a stiff leg for the rest of your life and that's the price you'll pay for behaving like an animal."

Longarm finished his work by wrapping the wound tight enough to staunch the flow of blood. Satisfied that he had done everything possible, he went outside and washed his hands in a horse trough, then went next door to a saloon and ordered whiskey.

"You're new in town, aren't you?" the bartender asked.

"That's right."

"I suppose you came to find work."

"Nope." Longarm took the bottle. "I'm just passing through."

"Where you heading?"

"I don't know," Longarm said honestly.

The bartender gave him a quizzical look, then shook his head. "Well, a tumbleweed has to roll whichever way the wind blows."

Longarm agreed. He paid for his bottle of whiskey and

then went back to the jail. Longarm spent ten minutes searching for a key to the cell and when he came up empty, he said to hell with it, figuring that his prisoner was not about to escape given his ruined knee.

The long journey down from Elko in that stagecoach had taken the steam out of Longarm. He was bone-tired, and after he had a drink and a nap, he needed to inquire as to just how long he might have to wait before a circuit judge came through Whiskey Creek.

But then it hit him—what if a judge *never* came through this town?

Longarm scowled. He tried to think of what he would do with the prisoner. About the only thing he could do was to find someone in Whiskey Creek with enough guts and integrity to agree to fill the late Marshal York's boots. And if no one could be found, he'd have to either transport this prisoner back to Elko to stand trial, or else turn him loose.

Neither option was much to Longarm's liking. He poured himself a stiff drink and took a seat in the late Marshal York's chair. He kicked his boots up on the desktop and leaned back, looking out through a bullet-shattered front window. He could hear men in the street shouting and shooting and raising billy-bob hell.

"How am I ever going to find a man with enough guts and ability to survive here?" he said to himself out loud.

Longarm dozed off with that very question foremost in his mind. He must have slept for at least two hours because when he woke up, the sun was down and the town was roaring. And when he looked back at the cell, his prisoner was gone.

Longarm's boots slammed down on the floor and he bolted out of his chair. "Sonofabitch!" he exclaimed, staring at the wide-open door.

The man was gone without a trace, but Longarm knew for sure that he had not escaped under his own power. Someone must have come and carried him out, probably while he was still unconscious, or else he would have howled with pain and Longarm would have been rudely awakened.

Longarm was embarrassed. He knew that it was only a matter of time before he found his escaped prisoner, but that did not ease the sense of failure he felt for allowing his prisoner to be whisked away while he was caught napping.

It was time to eat. Longarm knuckled the sleep from his eyes and grabbed his coat. He supposed that he was damned lucky that whoever had absconded with his prisoner had not been in a murderous frame of mind. Otherwise, he himself might be dead.

"I'll find him later," Longarm said out loud, deciding that he would enjoy a good meal and a night's sleep at his hotel, then bright and early go over to the Flatrock Livery and see what kind of a horse he could buy from the fella named Duncan.

But no miserable mustang. Uh-uh, not for United States Deputy Marshal Custis Long.

Chapter 4

Longarm came to a stop in the cluttered yard of the Flatrock Livery. "Is your name Duncan?"

"Yep."

The old man was sitting on an empty nail keg out in front of his livery. Longarm could see that the keg had been moved around quite often because it had stamped a lot of rings in the dirt. Now, he was about to see why the keg kept moving as the old man gleefully spat on a red ant, drenching it with tobacco juice. The ant quivered and stopped struggling, and the old man's eyes began to rake the earth searching for another victim.

"Here," Longarm said, handing Duncan the note he'd been given by the bartender. "It says—"

"I kin read."

Longarm watched as the man's lips moved slowly. Duncan was in his seventies and had a wide rack of shoulders and a massive head covered with white curls. His skin was dark-complected, and he had a pair of the biggest, gnarliest hands that Longarm had ever seen. It took Duncan a long time to read the short note and when he was finished, he folded it up very neatly and put it into his pocket, as careful as if it were big money.

"You an outlaw or a lawman?"

"What makes you think I'm either?"

"You ain't no miner and you ain't no farmer. Your hands are too rough to belong to a gambler, and besides, you've spent a lot of time in the sun."

"Is that all?"

"Nope. I can tell you're not a working cowboy because you don't have the rolling walk and your boots have low heels without spurs."

"You're a very observant man," Longarm said with more than a little admiration. He reached into his shirt pocket and retrieved his badge. "I am a lawman but I was told not to advertise the fact."

"Damned good advice. So what kind of a horse do you need?"

"A sound one with good wind and speed."

"You're hunting men?"

Longarm hesitated, then nodded his head. "I am. Three of them that robbed a bank in Elko and killed a bank manager as well as a couple of the customers. Pete saw them come through town and leave again."

"Describe 'em."

Longarm begin to describe the three killers, and before he was even through, Duncan nodded. "I recollect seein' them three. They were a hard-lookin' bunch, all right. Had damned good horses too. One was riding a palomino gelding. A flashy bastard that I'd have paid plenty to own. The other two were riding bay geldings, real handsome ones."

"That's why I have to be equally well mounted," Longarm said. "When I overtake them, I have to be able to close in to make the arrest."

"Or kill 'em."

"Yes," Longarm agreed. "Or kill them. It's their choice to make, not mine."

"Three against one is long odds," Duncan said, studying Longarm through squinted eyes.

"They are, except I have one big advantage."

The old man had been about to spit again at a new ant. Instead, he looked up sharply. "And that is?"

"I *know* I'm coming, but they don't."

Duncan cackled. "I like your attitude," he said. "If'n I was forty years younger, I'd ride along with you just to see how good you are, Mr. Lawman."

"So far, I've been good enough to stay alive." Longarm pulled a chomped-off cheroot from his vest pocket. "What about a good horse?"

"I got some out around back that will knock your eyes out."

"Fine, but no mustangs."

"What the hell you got against mustangs?" Duncan asked, drenching yet another hapless red ant.

"I never saw one that had any size to him. And while they might be broken, they're not trustworthy."

"Mr. Lawman, I aim to prove you wrong. So just hold on to your reservations long enough to look and listen. Is that fair enough?"

"I expect," Longarm said. "But I never saw a rattlesnake or a mustang that I admired."

"At least half of that is about to change," the old man said as he sort of leaned forward off the keg and rolled into a stiff motion.

"You walk pretty stove up," Longarm said.

Duncan turned and grimaced. "If you'd have busted as many broncs as I have and were my age, you'd hobble too."

Feeling a little dressed down, and deservedly so, Longarm followed the gimpy old man around the barn. They weaved their way through a bunch of broken-down wagons, and came upon a large corral where a remuda of tall Thoroughbred-looking roan horses stood watching them.

"Where are the mustangs?"

"You're looking at 'em."

"These strawberry roans?"

"Yep."

"I don't believe it," Longarm said with a shake of his head.

"Believe it or not, it's the truth," Duncan replied. "About six years ago, a rich fella brought a Thoroughbred stallion through these parts. The horse's name was The Red Devil and he was a runnin' fool. Anyway, he'd already beaten everything back East when he pulled a tendon, which ended his racing career. A few of the local ranchers were smart enough to buy that stallion. They figured to breed him to their better-grade mares and raise a superior line of horses for their cowboys."

"But The Red Devil escaped," Longarm said, guessing the end to this story.

"That's right. He broke out of a pole corral and headed for the Ruby Mountains. Turned out he'd pretty much healed that tendon problem. Healed it well enough so that nothing the cowboys could ride would overtake him on the run. The rest is local history."

Longarm stepped over to the corral and laid his arms over its top rail. "So these are his progeny, huh?"

"What's that?"

"His sons and daughters."

"That's right." Duncan nodded. "The Red Devil had a champion's blood, and even though his mares were your normal undersized mustangs, his offspring turned out to be exceptional animals. They've got a Thoroughbred's size and speed and they've got the stamina and brains of the mustang. Marshal, these are outstanding horses."

Longarm was about halfway convinced. He studied the roans and liked everything about them. They were big horses, most about sixteen hands tall and weighing eleven to twelve hundred pounds. They were like no other mustangs that Longarm had ever seen, and he credited that fact to the escaped Thoroughbred stallion.

"What ever happened to The Red Devil?"

"The mustang killers finally got him. The Red Devil got old and all that racin' he did back East gave him arthritis."

Duncan spat and pointed in the direction of the distant mountains. "I saw him once on a cold winter day and I could see how stiff he was in the joints. He moved like I do. Stiff and slow. I tried to catch him, but The Red Devil was too smart and got into some bad brush and rocks. Next year, a bullet found him."

"For the hide and tail?"

"That's right. The mustang killers skinned The Red Devil out, and they even brought his head into town seeing as how that horse had gotten so famous. When folks learned what they'd done to that famous horse, they were damned upset and we almost had a big shootout in the street."

"From what I've seen," Longarm said drily, "that wouldn't be any big news. Whiskey Creek is lawless."

"Wasn't always that'a way." Duncan sighed. "We've had some good lawmen over the years and . . . well, maybe I shouldn't be tellin' a federal marshal this, but when things got out of hand, we had a few necktie parties."

"So what happened to the town?"

"The miners took it over," Duncan said. "All the gold and silver brought in the worst kinds of folks. It's been downhill ever since."

"Then why stay?"

"Got nowhere else to go," Duncan answered. "Besides, I like spittin' on ants and talkin' to strangers that come through town. And I like my roan mustangs."

Longarm turned his attention back to the band of red horses. "Are any of them broke to ride?"

Duncan looked pained. "Dammit, of course they are! I broke 'em all."

"You?" Longarm put a smile on his lips. "No offense, but you don't look capable of climbing onto a horse, much less bucking one out."

The old man sighed. "I do a lot of my breaking on the

ground. I use lead lines to teach them to stop, back up, and to respond to the rein. It's easy but it takes a lot longer. I got the time and the patience now that I didn't have in my wild workin' days. I spend a few hours a day ground-breaking horses and by the time that I'm finished, they don't even think about bucking."

"I'd enjoy seeing you work," Longarm said, meaning it. "Unfortunately, I've got to go after those three bank robbers before their trail gets any colder."

"You'll catch 'em on one of these red horses," Duncan vowed. "Just get them in sight and you'll run 'em down. That's a promise, Marshal."

"How much money are you asking for one?"

Duncan scrubbed his whiskered chin. "Well, since I paid a hell of a lot to have my Paiute Indian friends catch these horses and geld the yearling colts, I can't let one of 'em go cheap."

"How much?"

"The mares are higher because I plan on breeding them back to a Thoroughbred, if I ever find one that I can buy at the right price."

"I'd rather have a gelding. One like that handsome fella with the flaxen mane and tail standing off a little to himself on the right."

"You've got a good eye," Duncan said as a compliment. "That's the pick of the lot. I'd have to have a hundred dollars for him."

"That's way too much. I work for the federal government, remember? I don't make a lot of money."

"How much will you make extra if you capture or kill them bank robbers?"

"Not a cent."

"Not even if they still have some of that Elko bank money left in their pockets?"

"Not even," Longarm said.

Duncan frowned. "I guess I could let you have that big

gelding for seventy-five dollars—if you'd be willing to sell him back to me for fifty dollars after you've caught your men."

"So why don't you just rent the animal to me for twenty-five dollars?"

"Because I think you'll want to keep him," Duncan said.

"That's not likely. I work out of Denver and quite often I travel by train and then rent a horse. It saves the government money and I don't have to worry about the expense of feeding an animal or having it hauled by rail all over the West. It's a lot cheaper."

"You get about what you pay for in life," Duncan said. "If you rent cheap horses you ride cheap horses."

"I rent the best horseflesh that I can find."

"Not from me you don't," Duncan said. "If you buy a horse, you always take good care of him. That's why you got to buy a horse from me, Marshal. And to buy that big, handsome red horse you spied over yonder is going to cost you seventy-five dollars."

"You're a tough man to do business with, Duncan," Longarm said. "Does the seventy-five include a saddle, bridle, and blanket?"

"Hell, no!"

"And how much extra would that cost?"

"Twenty-five for everything."

"So," Longarm said. "We're back to a hundred dollars."

"That's right. Take it or leave it."

"I want to see you ride that gelding before I decide."

"I'll do 'er."

And he did. The old man found a bridle and went into the corral, where he collected the red gelding. He led the animal out of the pen, and then he saddled and bridled it while Longarm looked on with admiration. When it came time to mount the horse, Duncan had Longarm get him a little stepladder, which he climbed and then used to ease himself into the saddle. All the while, the handsome roan stood quiet.

"What'd I tell you?" Duncan crowed.

"Ride him around the corral a little," Longarm ordered. "I want to see how he moves."

"He moves like a young woman, smooth and pretty," Duncan said as he began to ride the gelding back and forth.

On the ground, Duncan was a busted-up old man. On a horse, he was high, wide, and handsome. The old man sat straight, and you could have put an egg on his hat brim and it wouldn't have moved, not even at a trot. Longarm saw a change in Duncan's expression as well as his entire demeanor. He seemed younger, almost happy, as he rode the gelding back and forth.

"If you want to open that gate, I'll gallop him up and down in the street."

Longarm had seen enough. He wanted this horse in the worst way. Almost, and it embarrassed him to admit it, almost the way he wanted a woman. The horse was just that flat-out extraordinary.

"Sold!" Longarm shouted.

Duncan nodded in agreement. "Open the gate and we'll take him into the barn. I've got a fella that will shoe him for five dollars."

"You're not throwing in shoes?"

"Hell, no!"

Longarm grinned. "No matter. I'll take him anyway."

"I knew you would," Duncan said. "How soon are you leaving?"

"Just as soon as I can find my escaped prisoner and someone to watch over him."

Duncan stopped smiling. "You took a prisoner?"

"I did. One that attacked Mrs. York. Didn't you hear that I shot a couple of men?"

Duncan wasn't listening. He reined the mustang back

over to the ladder and eased himself out of the saddle, then down the ladder.

"So," Longarm continued after he finished telling the story, "it might be a few days before I can find someone to fill in at the marshal's office."

"It'll take a few years, likely," the liveryman said. "If you wait around to find someone dumb enough to become the local constable, we'll all die of old age first."

Longarm chuckled. "I take that to mean that you haven't anyone in mind that would consent to become marshal?"

"Not unless he's drunk or loco."

"I'll find someone," Longarm vowed.

Duncan just shook his head. "Better unsaddle and bridle that horse and turn him loose back in the corral with his brothers and sisters. It'll be a good long while before you head off on the outlaw trail."

Longarm started to protest, but Duncan turned and shuffled away. Maybe, Longarm thought, finding someone to become the marshal of Whiskey Creek was going to be even harder than he'd first thought.

Chapter 5

Longarm bellied up to the bar and motioned to Pete for a whiskey. The owner of the Wildcat Waterhole strolled over polishing a glass. He plunked it down hard on the bar top and asked, "Did old Duncan sell you a mustang?"

"Hell, yes," Longarm said a little sheepishly. "I never seen the likes of his mustangs."

"I should have told you about that old stallion. The Red Devil. The truth of the matter is that we have an especially high grade of mustangs in these parts."

"And yet you people allow men to shoot them for their hides and tails?"

Pete hadn't been expecting a comment like that, and he appeared injured when he said, "I own a saloon and I ain't got time to worry about happens out on the range."

"Yeah," Longarm said, taking up his drink. "I expect that's right." They talked a bit more, and Longarm revealed who he was and mentioned the prisoner who had escaped. "Who does the doctoring in Whiskey Creek?" he asked.

"The undertaker, Pendergast. He also pulls teeth and has even been known to deliver babies."

"Where can I find this Pendergast fella?"

"About six doors up the street. You'll see his shop with a striped barber pole outside, and when you go in, he has a barber and dentist chair. You can't miss it."

"Thanks."

"Good luck finding your prisoner," Pete said before he moved on down the bar.

Longarm nodded, and it did not take two minutes before he was opening the front door of the Pendergast's combination barber, dentist, and undertaker's shop. In Longarm's experience, most men in these lines of work were pale and not especially hearty fellows. Pendergast, it would seem, was definitely the exception. He stood well over six feet tall, a strapping and muscular fellow in his late thirties.

"Hello there!" he said heartily as he laid a magazine down and came to his feet. "Stranger in town, aren't you?"

"I am."

"Haircut and a shave?"

Longarm removed his Stetson, ran his fingers through his long and tangled hair, then scratched at his heavy stubble. "Sure. Why not?"

"It'll make a man feel taller, cleaner, and more prosperous," Pendergast assured him. "It will also turn a lady's eye to see such a handsome man as yourself all slicked up and smellin' good."

Longarm allowed himself a smile as he eased into the barber and dentist's chair. "Pete over at the Wildcat tells me that you are a man of many talents. He says you also pull teeth, doctor folks, and serve as the town's undertaker."

"Yes, I do," Pendergast said cheerily. "In a town as wild and wooly as Whiskey Creek, business is usually pretty good. We bury about two men a month, and I treat about three times that many for gunshot and knife wounds."

"I see."

"How are your teeth?" Pendergast asked.

"They're just fine."

"Want me to take a look at them after your shave?

Won't cost you anything unless I have to pull some. Ain't nothing worse than a toothache, and I can see 'em coming and pull the bad ones first."

"No, thank you."

Pendergast shrugged and draped Longarm, then wasted no time with the scissors. "You got a good thick head of hair, mister. You sure don't have to worry about ever going bald."

"Thanks."

"Now, I expect that I'll go bald someday. My father was completely bald by the time he was forty and my hair is thinning fast. My wife teases me that she can see the back of my head shine in lamplight." Pendergast laughed.

"Actually," Longarm said, "I did need more than a shave and haircut."

The scissors momentarily stopped clipping. "How can I help you?"

"I am a United States deputy marshal headquartered in Denver, Colorado."

"You don't say?"

"I do say. I'm looking for three men that robbed the Elko bank and shot several innocent people to death." Longarm quickly described them. "Maybe you've seen them here lately?"

"I have. Tough characters even in a town like Whiskey Creek. But I haven't seen them in, oh, about a week."

"I heard they've left town," Longarm said. "There's another fella I'm looking for. I shot him in the back of the legs, and then I doctored him in the marshal's office and left him in a cell."

"I see." The scissors clipped faster.

"Have you seen him?"

Pendergast cleared his throat nervously. "I don't suppose that you have any identification, do you?"

"Of course." Longarm pulled out his badge and showed it to the man. "Do you want more?"

"No, that will do."

"Were you called upon to treat my prisoner that escaped yesterday afternoon?"

"What did he do?"

Longarm could have gotten riled by the question, but he decided to answer. "He and two other animals were just about to rape Mrs. York when I broke up their fun. I shot two of them to death in the alley, but the third one broke and ran. I put a couple of bullets into his legs and dragged him off to jail."

"That isn't what they told me when they brought the bodies in yesterday," Pendergast said. "I was told that it was just another fight between men."

"Not true." Longarm relaxed. "Go ahead and finish up the haircut since you've already started. But I'll come back for the shave after I return my prisoner to jail. Now, where is my wounded prisoner?"

"He was brought in and his wounds were bleeding. I bandaged him up and his friends carried him off."

"Do you know where?"

"They're staying at the Cedar Hotel."

"I know where that is," Longarm said. "In your opinion, will the prisoner survive his wounds?"

"Yes! But his knee is shattered and he'll never walk again without considerable pain. He was pretty damned bitter about that and so were his friends. You see, he won't be able to make a living any more in the mines."

"He should have thought about that before he tried to rape Mrs. York."

"How is she?"

Longarm shrugged. "She seemed okay. I have the feeling that she'd have shot the last man herself if I had given her my gun."

"Donita York is a damned strong woman. I don't know why she hasn't left Whiskey Creek. I think she is trying to sell her home for money to get a start elsewhere."

"I hope she sells pretty quickly," Longarm said. "I can't imagine a woman as pretty as she is living alone in this rough and lawless town."

"Someday we'll have law."

"Yeah," Longarm replied. "And I hope it's a lot sooner than you expect. I'm looking for a lawman. I have the authority—and responsibility—to ensure that law and order are maintained. I don't suppose you'd be—"

"Oh, no!" Pendergast exclaimed. "I'll stick to a healthy line of work. I'd rather bury folks than be buried."

"I understand. Does anyone come to mind that might be willing and able to step into the marshal's office? I'd be willing to stick with him for a few days to get him off to a good start."

"Can't think of a soul," Pendergast said. "I really can't. Marshal York was smart and tough, but look what happened to him. No, sir, I don't think you'll find a good man to take a badge in Whiskey Creek."

Longarm frowned. "Well," he said, "I *have* to find someone and pretty quick. So after I recapture my prisoner, I'll make that my first order of business."

"Good luck."

"Thanks. More and more I'm realizing that I'll need it."

The Cedar Hotel was an establishment of the roughest order. It was dirty and smelled bad. There were a half-dozen miners lounging about on ripped sofas in the lobby, and they glared suspiciously at Longarm when he came in the door and walked up to the registration desk.

No one came out to help him, so Longarm removed his six-gun and hammered hard on the desk with the butt of his Colt until the desk clerk hurried out from behind a partition.

"Jeezus!" the clerk complained. "What is all the commotion about?"

"You've got a man staying here with shot-up legs. He's my escaped prisoner. Where is he?"

The clerk took a step back. "Mister, I . . . I don't know what you mean."

Longarm reached into his pocket, flashed his badge, and growled, "I'll throw you in the jail too if you don't tell me where to find my prisoner."

"Room Twelve," the man said quickly.

"What's his name?"

"Ike Moffit."

"Come along and open the door."

"Here, take the key. But don't kill him on the bed, for crissakes!"

Longarm ignored the plea. He marched up the hallway hearing the men in the lobby speaking in loud voices. No doubt they were upset at Longarm, but he did not care.

The door wasn't locked, and Longarm knocked it open with a bang. Ike Moffit was reaching for a six-gun draped over the edge of his bed when Longarm stopped him cold with the sound of his own cocking six-gun.

"I wouldn't do that if I were you, Ike."

The man twisted around, his face pure poison. "Why don't you just leave me the hell alone! I could have shot you before my friends carried me out of that cell. I let you live, by gawd!"

"And I appreciate that very much," Longarm said. "But it doesn't change the fact that you tried to rape a woman and that deserves punishment."

"Don't you think that being crippled is punishment enough?"

"That's for a judge and a jury to decide."

"You're a hard-assed sonofabitch, ain't ya."

"Get up," Longarm said.

"I can't walk!"

"Is that right?" Longarm went over and collected the man's six-gun and then said coldly, "You're going to jail either standing up or laying out. Now which is it going to be?"

"I . . . I'll need some help."

"All right."

Longarm helped the man to his feet and then out of the room. Ike Moffit was in considerable pain. When they reached the lobby, several of Ike's miner friends came over to stop Longarm, who said, "I'm a United States deputy marshal and this man is under arrest. If you try to interfere, boys, you'll be in big trouble."

"What the hell!" a man said. "Don't you think that Ike has paid enough?"

"I explained all that to him just a minute ago. I'm a lawman and this man is under arrest. A judge or a jury will decide what happens to him—not me and not you. So why don't you give your friend a hand to jail?"

They weren't happy, but they must have realized that Longarm wasn't bluffing, because they carried a grunting and grimacing Ike Moffit up the street and back into jail.

"Hey!" Longarm called before the grumbling miners exited the marshal's office. "Any of you boys know how to use a six-gun well enough to pin on a marshal's badge?"

The miners turned to glare at him, and one even dared to make an obscene gesture. "Well," Longarm said with a shrug, "I was just asking."

Once Longarm was alone with his prisoner at the marshal's office, Ike hollered, "Marshal, there isn't even a judge willing to come to Whiskey Creek, for gawdsakes! We could both rot in this hellhole waitin' for something to happen."

"No judge?"

"Not that I can remember."

"Hmm," Longarm mused. "But there is a stagecoach that arrives every day or two."

"Yeah, there's that."

"Well, then," Longarm said, "I'll get a letter to Elko

asking the authorities to send a judge *muy pronto*.''

"Shit!" Ike swore. "You are just bound and determined to send me off to prison, aren't you?"

"I think you deserve it," Longarm said. "You can't be much of a man if you'd join two others and take advantage of a young woman like Mrs. York."

"I told you she was just a damn breed!"

Longarm had been about to sit down, but Ike's words brought him over to the cell. "Mister, if you *were* repentant, I suppose that I might even be persuaded to feel sorry for you given your knee and the fact that you'll hobble for the rest of your life. But you sound to me like you'd do it all over again given half the chance."

"I would," Ike hissed. "She's a handsome and a lonely woman who—"

"Don't talk to me anymore," Longarm said with disgust. "I'm going to need to find someone to watch over you until the judge comes."

"Ain't no one foolish enough to do that. And I tell you something else, Mr. Marshal."

"And that is?"

"If my friends catch you nappin', we'll make sure you don't ever wake up again. You understand me?"

"Thanks for the warning, which only a fool would give," Longarm said as he started for the door.

"Hey, I'm hungry!"

Longarm turned and smiled. "Me too. That's why I'm going to eat."

"But . . . but what about me!"

"Maybe I'll bring you back my leftovers," Longarm replied with a cold smile. "If I don't see some skinny dog that looks hungry."

"You big, ornery sonofabitch! Someone in Whiskey Creek is going to gun you down!"

Longarm headed for the nearest café hearing his stomach growling.

"Excuse me!" a voice called.

Longarm turned to see Donita York. She was smiling and looked wonderful. There seemed to be no trace of bitterness or anger from the attack. Removing his Stetson, Longarm said, "Mrs. York, you look as pretty as a primrose."

She blushed and her dark eyelashes fluttered. When she spoke, it was with only a hint of a Spanish accent, although her dress and that turquoise jewelry made it plain that she was of mixed blood. Donita curtsied, lifting her pretty skirt just above her ankles. "You are a very brave man, Señor. I wish to invite you to my house for supper tonight."

"Aw," he said, waving his hand distractedly, "you don't have to go to all that trouble."

"It is no trouble, Señor, it is an honor."

Longarm felt his heart skip, and he wondered if she could read his thoughts and his desire. This was a beautiful woman, and Longarm realized that he would have to be very careful not to show her how much her beauty affected him. After all, she had only recently been widowed, and her man, bless his soul, had been a marshal.

"If you're sure that I'm not putting you out any, then I'd be pleased to join you for supper. As a matter of fact, I was just going out to find something to eat. I'm plenty hungry, Mrs. York."

"Donita," she said, taking his hand.

Longarm's big hand completely engulfed hers. "Yes, ma'am. I mean, Donita."

As they strolled along the boardwalk, Longarm was aware that men were staring at Donita with pure lust. A few muttered something under their whiskey breaths as he passed, but Longarm chose to ignore them, until one drunken miner about the size of a small horse decided to block their progress.

"Well, well," he said with a loose smile as his eyes

devoured Donita. "If it ain't Mrs. York huntin' herself up another lawman!"

"Watch your tongue," Longarm said, his hands clenching at his sides.

"I tell you where I'd like to *put* my tongue," the huge man said with a lascivious wink that brought a flush to Donita's cheeks. "I'd like to put it—"

Longarm's fist traveled less than eighteen inches before it exploded into the huge man's solar plexus and brought him up on his toes like an overstuffed ballerina. The giant's mouth formed a big oval, which Longarm filled with a straight left jab that sent the man crashing to the boardwalk.

"I'm sorry for that," Longarm said, holding a set of teeth-cut knuckles up for examination.

"You're going to need that hand bandaged," Donita said.

"I think these knuckles will heal just fine."

"I'm going to bandage them anyway," she said. "Otherwise, they might get infected. It would have been safer to be bitten by a dog than an animal like him."

"I can't argue that fact," Longarm said in full agreement as they continued down the boardwalk. Only now, there were no leers, crude whisperings, or bold looks directed at the widow that Longarm was escorting.

Donita lived at the far end of town in a tidy little clapboard house. It was humble, only two rooms, but it was about as nice as any lawman could expect given their poor pay.

"Something smells good," Longarm said after she had cleaned and bandaged his cut knuckles.

"Have a seat, please."

Longarm took a seat as Donita hurried into her kitchen. A few moments later, she appeared with a crystal decanter of good Kentucky bourbon. "Help yourself before dinner."

"Won't you join me?"

"In a minute."

Longarm thought the bourbon was as good as he'd tasted in a long, long time. The bourbon went down smooth and left a warm glow in the pit of his empty stomach. Longarm could feel it smolder, and he could hear Donita humming in her kitchen.

Coming to his feet, Longarm walked around the little dining room admiring the pictures and personal belongings of the household. He noticed a daguerreotype of Marshal York and Donita holding a wedding cake. They both looked very happy. Donita was wearing a simple white wedding dress and she appeared to be no more than sixteen years old.

"My husband was very handsome, no?"

"Yes," Longarm said, turning around. "How long were you married?"

"Six years." Donita's eyes misted. "We were very much in love, Señor. He was a good man, and like you, very handsome and very brave."

"I'm sorry he was killed," Longarm said awkwardly. "It happens all too often in this line of work. Did they ever find out who ambushed him?"

"No," she said, bitterness in her voice. "There were many men who would do it. This town is bad, Señor."

"My name is Custis."

"Custis."

Donita rolled the word off her red lips and made the name actually sound fine. "I like that. My husband's name was Donald."

"I see." Longarm felt a little uncomfortable, and so he moved around Donita and filled his glass, then raised it in a tribute. "To the memory of your late husband."

"Yes," she said, filling her own glass, "and to the day when his killer receives his eternal reward in Hell."

Longarm was surprised by the passion in her voice as they both tossed their whiskey down.

"Are you ready to eat?" she asked.

"I sure am!"

Donita had prepared Mexican dishes that night and they were wonderful. Tortillas, tamales, rice and beans, all heavily spiced the way he liked. For dessert, she fed him the most American dish of all, apple pie.

"I'm stuffed to the gills," he announced later that evening as they sat together on a lumpy horsehair couch. "I sure did enjoy your cooking, Donita."

"Then you will come back tomorrow night?"

"I'd like to do that, but I'm determined to leave Whiskey Creek as soon as I can. You see, I'm after three men that robbed a bank and murdered some good folks over in Elko."

"I understand," she said, not very successful in hiding her disappointment.

"But what I need to do before I go is to find someone to watch over my prisoner. The one that tried to . . . to hurt you."

Donita's black eyes sparked with sudden hatred. "I will watch over him for you."

"Uh . . . I don't think that would be such a good idea," he said. "I mean, I need someone that will not only watch him, but will also make sure that he is alive when a circuit judge finally shows up."

"In truth," she admitted, "I would probably shoot him."

"That's what I thought."

Donita gazed into Longarm's eyes. "Custis. May I speak to you boldly?"

"Boldly? Why, sure."

"Do you find me . . . pretty?"

"More than pretty. I think you're a beautiful woman. Very beautiful."

She moved a little closer. "It has been a long time since I have seen a man as brave and handsome as my husband."

Longarm felt a trickle of sweat dribble down his backbone. He was intoxicated, but it had nothing to do with that good Kentucky bourbon. "A long time, huh?"

"Too long."

He was trying to remind himself that she was the widow of a lawman slain in the line of duty, but all Longarm could think of was the way Donita's hair shone in the candlelight and the smell of her perfume and how her red lips seemed moist and so very inviting.

The next thing Longarm knew, Donita was climbing all over him. They tumbled off the couch to roll on the floor, kissing and pulling at each other's clothing. Donita was as fierce and as savage as a puma and just about as strong. Somehow, she had Longarm's gunbelt off and his pants down before he could even remove her skirt.

"This floor is mighty hard," he breathed, as she stood up and yanked his boots and then his pants completely off. "Don't you think it would be better if. . . . aw, hell, never mind."

She squatted on top of him even as she was yanking off the last of her undergarments. It happened so fast that Longarm wasn't sure if he was even physically prepared to enter her, but he was pleasantly surprised.

Donita mounted him and threw her head forward. All that lovely black hair cascaded over Longarm's face, and his lips found her lush breasts. He sucked on them as if they were ripe, sweet grapes.

She groaned and spread her legs wide, then began to bounce up and down on his manhood. Longarm groaned with pleasure, although he was wishing that he hadn't eaten such a big meal, and he hoped the beans weren't going to cause him embarrassment.

He needn't have worried. As Donita's body played expertly with Longarm's body, all his worries were replaced by waves of pleasure that rolled over them both like breakers on a wide, sandy beach.

"Oh, Señor Custis," she panted, "you are *muy hombre*. I like you very much!"

"The feeling is mutual," he grunted, rolling over on top of her and pistoning his big rod in and out until she arched her back and begged him to go slower but even deeper.

Longarm obliged. He pushed himself up on his arms and gazed down at her beautiful face. "You're quite a woman," he said, feeling a river of fire coursing through his body.

"Oh," she groaned, "don't stop too soon. *Please* don't stop too soon!"

Longarm played the woman as a musician would a violin. And when they reached their frantic crescendo, they were like cymbals crashing together in a rapturous frenzy.

Longarm rolled off the beautiful woman and gazed up at the ceiling, trying to catch his breath. She draped herself across his chest, black eyes still glazed with pleasure.

"Will you stay for breakfast, Señor?"

Longarm thought of his hungry prisoner, for about two seconds, and then he said, "You bet I will."

It was a night to remember, and by the time Longarm was able to drag himself out of Donita's bed and her passionate embrace, he felt as if he'd been riding broncs for a solid week.

"You are walking a little funny," Donita said with soft laughter. "Are you all right, hombre?"

"I just need a little rest," he said sheepishly.

"But you will be back tonight?"

"Yeah," he said, thinking he was going to need to find a bathtub and soak. "I wouldn't miss it. What are we having for supper tonight?"

"Each other," she said, eyes smoking.

"Uh . . . good," he managed to say as he left Donita at the doorstep.

Longarm still had a weary smile on his lips when he reached the marshal's office. He opened the door, and came face-to-face with a lean man with a boyish face and the coldest gray eyes imaginable.

"Who are you?" Longarm asked.

"My name is Billy Wade," he said, intently studying Longarm. "And I understand that you need the services of a tough professional marshal."

"That's right," Longarm said, aware of how thrashed he must appear in contrast to this handsome man in his early twenties. "But you look a little young for the part."

Wade shrugged. He was about six feet tall and lean. He had boyish good looks and was well dressed, and Longarm had him pegged as a gambler.

"I've been around some," he said. "I worked for Marshal Hatfield in Abilene, Kansas, and for Marshal Locke in Santa Fe. I heard that this was a hard town in need of a marshal, so I came to look it over. Then I heard about you."

"I see." Longarm walked past the young man and went over to collapse in his desk chair.

"Marshal Long, isn't it?"

"That's right."

"You look as if you've been up for about three hard nights running. Doesn't surprise me, though. It's going to take some doing to whip this town into shape."

"And you think you can help me do that?"

"I'm sure of it," Wade said with a confident grin. "Want to step out around back and see how I can handle a gun?"

"No," Longarm said, trying but failing to stifle a yawn. "I think right now, if you don't mind, I'm going to get some sleep."

Wade frowned. "What am I supposed to do?"

"Watch the front door and the prisoner. Make sure that no one wakes me up before noon," Longarm ordered as he kicked his boots up on the desk and tipped his hat forward over his eyes.

Chapter 6

‘‘Marshal Long?’’

Longarm roused in his desk chair. He opened his eyes to study the young man. ‘‘You still here?’’

‘‘I am.’’ Billy Wade frowned, then smoothed his dark, pencil-thin mustache. ‘‘I think we’d better have a talk.’’

‘‘All right,’’ Longarm said, knuckling sleep from his bloodshot eyes. ‘‘What about?’’

‘‘Hiring me as the marshal of Whiskey Creek.’’

‘‘Oh, yeah.’’ Longarm yawned. ‘‘Billy, what makes you think that you can survive in this town when every marshal before you has been shot to death or run out with his tail tucked between his legs?’’

‘‘Watch,’’ Billy said, hand flashing toward his six-gun.

If Longarm had blinked, he would have missed the young man’s fast draw. Billy’s hand was a blur as it flashed to his Colt, which came up smooth and fast before it stopped rock-steady in his fist.

Billy twirled his gun back into his holster. He folded his arms across his chest and said, ‘‘What do you think?’’

‘‘I think you’re a show-off.’’

‘‘No, I’m not!’’ Billy exclaimed. ‘‘I’m a professional lawman. Like you. But I’m looking for a reputation and

Whiskey Creek will give it to me. You won't find another taker, so what do you say?"

Longarm came to his feet and arched his aching back. He studied the earnest young man. "You say that you've worked in Abilene and Santa Fe?"

"That's right. They're pretty rough towns too, but I proved my worth."

"You got a letter of recommendation to back up that claim?"

"I do."

He extracted two letters from inside his coat pocket and handed them to Longarm, who read them quickly. Both letters were from the town marshals of Abilene and Santa Fe and were extremely laudatory. They said that Billy Wade was courageous, very cool under fire, and resourceful. They recommended Billy for any position he might want.

"What do you think?"

Longarm handed them back to the intent young man. "They look just fine to me. How long did you work at each of those places?"

"Two years in Abilene and eighteen months in Santa Fe."

"And why did you leave?"

Billy shrugged. "I just got restless. I guess that's my problem. Once I sort of feel that I've got things under control, then I get the itch to move along."

"Nothing so wrong with that," Longarm said. "As a matter of fact, that's one of the reasons that I'm a United States deputy marshal instead of a local marshal or sheriff. I like the challenge of going to new places and straightening out things."

Billy grinned. "If I do a good job here, maybe you'd be willing to recommend me to whoever it is that hired you."

"Maybe," Longarm said. "But I am a little concerned about your somewhat brief experience. I'm told that the worst element of this town likes nothing better than to humiliate a lawman and then send him to the cemetery packed in a pine box.''

"I expect that might take some doing in your case,'' Billy said without looking a bit worried, "as it would in mine.''

"I really don't have the authority to hire you,'' Longarm admitted. "However, as a United States marshal, I will recommend to the county authorities that they must establish law and order in this town.''

"Does your recommendation carry any weight?''

Longarm chuckled. "Actually, it does. You see, there are federal laws that supersede the state and territorial laws. For example, if Nevada wanted to denounce its statehood, the federal government would come in and put an immediate end to that nonsense.''

"I see,'' Billy mused. "And what would this Whiskey Creek job pay?''

"I have no idea, but I expect about forty dollars a month would be tops. The starting pay might be as low as thirty dollars a month and found.''

"That's not much,'' Billy said. "In Abilene and Santa Fe both, I got considerably more.''

"But no reputation.''

"Yeah,'' Billy said. "And that was okay then, but it isn't now. It's time that I become number one.''

"Number one, huh?''

"That's right.''

Longarm wasn't sure that he liked the way Billy was thinking, but he did admire a man with ambition. "Well,'' he said, "number one in a small town like this isn't a big deal. In the larger towns, the marshal is often elected. Mostly, though, the town councils choose their constables. I doubt that Whiskey Creek even has a town council.''

"Then that would be one of the first things I'd recommend we form,'' Billy said, hooking his thumbs in his gunbelt. ''And I'd ask them to pay me a salary equal to the risks I'd be taking to clean up this hellhole.''

Longarm couldn't help but be impressed by this young man. He seemed a little naive, but there was also a steely nerve and a confidence in his manner that said a lot about his abilities. Longarm had seen Billy handle a gun, and there was little doubt that the young man was as accurate as he was quick. But still, his lack of experience was troubling. The last thing Longarm wanted to do was to leave an inexperienced although idealistic young man in this office who would go out and get himself killed in the line of duty.

''Listen,'' Billy said, ''I can read your thoughts and you're worried that I'm biting off more than I can chew.''

''You got that right,'' Longarm admitted. ''This is a tough town and it'd be a challenge for anyone to tame.''

''Even you?''

''Even me.''

''I doubt that,'' Billy said. ''I've asked around town and you've already made quite an impact. People are talking about what you did to those three that tried to take advantage of the Widow York. I'd say that you believe in swift justice, Marshal Long, and I admire that.''

''Not so swift for that one in the cell,'' Longarm commented, glancing at Ike Moffit. ''I'm surprised that he hasn't been yelling for food.''

''I guess Ike understands that we won't tolerate that,'' Billy said. ''I had a little talk with him before you came, and he sort of come to realize that we're not going to coddle him and his every need.''

Longarm raised his eyebrows. ''A little talk?''

''That's right. In Abilene, we wouldn't stand for our prisoners swearing or pissing on the floor or any of that low behavior. We made them understand that they were to mind their manners and keep their mouths shut.''

''Sounds good. But what if they told you to go to hell?''

Billy shrugged with indifference. "Then we'd just have to have a little heart-to-heart talk with them, Marshal Long. That's really all there was to it."

"I see. And you had a little 'heart-to-heart talk' with Ike, did you?"

"I did." Billy winked. "After I explained the new rules that I set, and after he understood them completely, our prisoner became very cooperative."

Longarm walked over to the cell and stared through the bars. "Ike?"

Moffit had been lying on his hard bunk facing the wall. He turned and glanced at Longarm, then turned back to the wall muttering, "Leave me alone!"

"We'll get you something to eat before long."

Moffit didn't say anything.

Longarm shook his head. "Billy, you sure taught him the beauty of silence. He was pretty foulmouthed when I locked him up again."

"I've no use for a man that would mistreat a woman, even a halfbreed woman."

"I'm glad to hear that," Longarm said a little stiffly, "because I sure feel the same way."

Billy grinned. "I hear that Mrs. York is a real beauty."

"She is."

"Too bad about her husband. She have any children?"

"No." Longarm went back to the desk and sat down, not wanting to talk about Donita's personal life with this handsome but cocky young man.

"I guess I'll be paying her my respects after I pin on her husband's badge."

"Whatever," Longarm said. "But until you get some authority from either the county sheriff's office or a town council that does not yet even exist, about the best I can do is to put in for some temporary pay to keep you in beans while you watch over this prisoner. The authorities should arrive from Elko within the week."

Billy looked surprised. "You've already sent for them?"

"I'll send a letter with today's stage explaining the situation here and telling them about you. I expect that you'll be hearing from the marshal over in Elko soon enough. Until then, you might want to leave Marshal York's badge in his desk drawer and just play the role of jailer."

"Thanks," Billy said. "I appreciate your recommendation and all your good advice. You're exactly the kind of lawman that I'd like to be myself some day. And I hope that we might both wear a federal marshal's badge before too much time passes."

Longarm was flattered by this simple but heartfelt declaration. "Well, Billy," he said, "I just don't want to see you bite off more than you can swallow."

"I haven't." Billy took off his hat and combed his long curly hair with his fingers. "So when will you be leaving to go after those Elko bank robbers and shooters?"

"You heard about them, did you?"

"Sure. I met Pete over at the Wildcat."

"He's a talker."

"He said that you bought a damned fine mustang yesterday and were anxious to get after those bank robbers. That's why I was real surprised when you took a long nap today."

"I had a rough night."

"What was her name?"

Longarm found a cheroot to jam into the corner of his mouth. "A gentlemen," he said, "never tells."

Billy grinned. "A gentlemen doesn't spend the night screwing a supposedly grieving marshal's pretty halfbreed widow."

Longarm's eyes narrowed and his voice chilled. "Billy," he said, struggling to keep his voice civil, "you may think that you know everything, but you've got plenty yet to learn. And because you're young, I'll make an allowance in this case. But don't ever speak of Mrs. York again in my presence or refer to her as a halfbreed. Is that real clear?''

Billy paled, although Longarm did not know if it was from anger or fright. Maybe it was a little of both. Whatever, he stiffly nodded and went outside to get some fresh air. Longarm chewed on his cheroot a moment, wondering if he'd been too hard and why he cared so much about what people said or thought about Donita. Perhaps she had gotten under his skin a little more than he was willing to admit.

And perhaps, Longarm thought, a gentleman really should not screw a dead marshal's grieving widow, even when she wanted him to.

Longarm returned to his hotel room and gathered his belongings. On his way outside, the desk clerk called, ''Marshal Long, I hope you get your ass shot off by them bank robbers!''

Longarm paused and then slowly twisted around, debating if he should go back inside and have a word with that cheeky little sonofabitch. But when the man ducked behind the desk like a frightened rabbit, Longarm decided to just let the unkind remark ride.

Slamming the door on his way out, Longarm went directly over to see Donita. She was out in the back washing lots of clothes.

''Hi,'' he said, noting how her dress was soaked with perspiration from working over the steaming tubs of water. ''I'd never have imagined that you had so much laundry.''

''Hi yourself. How do you think I make a living in Whiskey Creek now that Donald is gone?''

''I hadn't thought of it,'' he admitted.

''Just like a man,'' she said, only there was no anger or accusation in her voice. ''I take in laundry and it pays my bills. My house is up for sale and when I find a buyer, I'm leaving this awful place.''

"I can understand that."

Donita looked flushed with the work and the heat. "I'm almost finished," she said. "Why don't you rest on the porch and I'll be along in a few minutes. We can have a drink and then I'll start dinner. I see you've got your saddlebags and satchel. Are you moving in with me?"

"No, but I would like to spend another night with you," he said, deciding to tell her that he was leaving town after they ate and made love.

Longarm made himself at home on Donita's porch. Donald York's rocking chair was comfortable and it was a fine day. He watched Donita wash and hang the last of her laundry while the sun quickly dried the clothes already hanging. Donita was nice to watch. Her long black hair was pulled back into a no-nonsense bun and her dress was a little small above the waist, which was just fine as far as Longarm was concerned.

"You're a great one for watching someone else work, aren't you Marshal?" she called.

"Would you like me to come and help?" He started to rise from the chair, but she motioned him to sit back down.

"Don't move! With your big hands you'd probably spill my fresh wash onto the dirt and I've have to redo it. I'm doing just fine."

"You sure are."

"What do you want for supper?"

"You," Longarm said as he pulled a cheroot out of his vest pocket. "And then we'll take a bath in that washtub you're using."

She giggled. "It's even dirtier than I am right now."

"I'll take my chances," Longarm bantered, enjoying himself immensely.

And so it went with them until after dinner and after another great session of lovemaking. Night fell quickly over this part of Nevada, and it wasn't until he'd had another taste of Donita that Longarm got around to telling her that he was leaving.

"Tomorrow morning!" she exclaimed, sitting up in bed and staring at him with eyes that said she did not want to believe his words.

"That's right." He pulled her to his side. "I'm a federal deputy marshal and there are three killers and bank robbers that I have to bring to justice."

"I know that, but why so soon?"

"I've been told that the men I seek are mustang hunters. Maybe they are and maybe they're not. All I can be sure of is that their trail grows colder with each passing hour."

"But I may never see you again!" Donita pressed her warm, soft body against Longarm. "If you wanted to stay, we could live here until I sold this place and then go away. We could make a life together."

"I can't do that," he said gently. "I've sworn to uphold the law. It's what I know and like to do."

"You'll get ambushed or gunned down someday," Donita said, pushing away. "You'll meet a younger, faster man with a gun. Or you'll ride into a trap or maybe—"

"Shhh," he ordered, placing a forefinger over her protesting lips. "I'm going to be just fine."

She pulled his hand away and her voice was pleading when she said, "Will you come back through Whiskey Creek when this is finished? Will you take me with you to Elko?"

"If you've sold this place and you're ready to leave, sure."

"And then on to Denver? I'd really like to see Denver, Custis. I'd like to see it with you, if you're not be ashamed to be seen by your friends in the company of a halfbreed."

"Don't say that," he ordered, drawing her to his side. "You're brave and beautiful. And I'd be proud and pleased to introduce you to all my friends and then escort you to all my favorite Denver haunts. My only concern is that I might be returning prisoners to justice and that would put you in some danger."

"I can take care of myself," she said. "Donald taught me how to use a gun, and I'm not half bad."

"I believe it."

"Do you?" She looked closely into his eyes. "Custis, you wouldn't lie about taking me to Denver, would you?"

"No," he heard himself say a moment before he kissed her lips and climbed back between her silken thighs. "I wouldn't lie. I'll take you with me to Denver."

Donita sighed with pleasure and relief. She opened herself wide and made him feel at home. Longarm lost track of the number of times they made love that night. All he knew for sure was they were so tired that the sun was fully up when there was a pounding at Donita's front door.

"Who is it?"

"Got some washing for you, Mrs. York."

"Just leave it by the front door."

There was a moment of silence, and then a disappointed voice said, "Oh, all right. If there's anything I can do for you, ma'am, all you got to do is ask."

"Who was that?" Longarm asked.

Donita stretched and then knuckled the sleep from her eyes. "I don't know."

Longarm grinned. "I suppose most every man in Whiskey Creek is anxious to get better acquainted with you."

"Maybe," she said, "but I'm a one-man woman and you're that one man."

Longarm was flattered, but also a little concerned. He sat up and ran his hands through his hair. "Donita," he told her, "I will be back. But that don't mean that I'm going to marry you or any such thing."

"Marry me?" She laughed. "Who said anything about marriage?"

"Well . . ."

She sat up and reached for him. "All I want from you

is what you can give me today. Is that plain enough?''

''It is,'' he said. ''But a woman like you deserves a husband.''

''And I'll have another someday. But not a lawman and not for a while. All right?''

''Sure.'' Longarm felt a little embarrassed and maybe even a little disappointed that she did not really want to be his wife.

He dressed quickly and went out to feed his horse, which he had put in Donita's little barn and corral. When he returned, breakfast was cooking and Donita was rushing around setting the table. He watched her, and was surprised to realize that she looked very happy.

''Are you really going to wait for me to come back for you?'' he asked.

She looked up from the table. ''That's right. We're going to Denver together, remember?''

''Of course.''

''Good,'' she said, ''now sit down while I get you some coffee and that breakfast.''

Longarm sat at her table and when he looked around at the little house and the pretty woman, it struck him quite forcibly that Marshal Donald York might have died young, but he'd probably died happy.

Chapter 7

"You look good on that big roan horse," Duncan said. "How do you like the saddle?"

"It's fine," Longarm replied, standing up in the stirrups. "It's a good outfit."

"Best hundred dollars you ever spent in your life," the liveryman proclaimed, spitting at a red ant, but missing. He furiously worked up another spit and followed the ant several feet before drenching him good. "Kin I give you some advice?"

"Of course."

Longarm patted the muscular neck of his tall roan gelding. He could feel the animal shiver with excitement and anticipation.

"These men you're hunting are supposed to be riding with them mustang killers. If that's true, you'd better be real careful because that bunch won't hesitate to put a bullet in you and that roan horse. And they're crack shots."

"I'm not too bad with a rifle myself."

"Maybe so, but you're at a hell of a disadvantage with that puny carbine. Those mustang killers carry big-caliber rifles. I'm thinking that you ought to have the same."

Longarm started to object, but Duncan turned around and hobbled into his barn, only to reappear a moment later with a Sharps .50-caliber center-fire breechloader, which was commonly referred to as a "Big Fifty."

"It's been converted from a percussion weapon by one of the finest gunsmiths in Nevada. Damn thing will drop a horse or buffalo at a thousand yards, if you could hit 'em."

"It's a beauty, but it's a single-shot," Longarm said, unable to hide his disappointment. "Won't do me much good against a bunch of hardcases if I get into a fight."

"Like hell it won't!" Duncan spat. "I'm giving you a bushel of 550-grain bullets that will give you more range and hitting power than their Remington buffalo rifles. If you're a marksman—and you'd damn well better be if you're going after that bunch—then you can empty two or three of their saddles with this Sharps before they even get into shootin' range."

"I'll sight it in this very afternoon."

"Sight it in, hell!" Duncan exclaimed. "It's already sighted in enough to blow off a gnat's ass at a hundred paces. You just keep it handy. Use your Winchester for the closer work, but don't forget that this Sharps is what might just save your bacon."

"I won't forget," Longarm promised, taking the rifle, which was sheathed in a special leather saddle boot. "It's too big a weapon to be ignored."

"You got food?"

Longarm slapped his saddlebags and the bedroll, frying pan, and cooking utensils he'd just bought with Donita's help. "I'm all set, Duncan."

The old man nodded. "I sure wish that I was young enough to go along. But I'd just slow you down and my eyes ain't good enough to shoot anything farther off than a hundred feet."

Longarm leaned forward a little. "Do me a favor, old-timer. Keep an eye on Donita . . . I mean Mrs. York. I'm a little worried about her."

"She looks sweeter than candy, but she's really tougher

than boot leather," Duncan said. "Don't be too worried about Donita, she's a fooler."

"I know, but keep an eye on her anyway, all right?"

"What about that fancy young fella that you're leaving to watch over the prisoner and our jail?"

"I think he'll be fine," Longarm said. "I got a feeling that he's pretty tough himself."

"Did you really make him our new marshal?"

"All I did was use my federal authority to put him in charge of watching over Ike Moffit, my wounded prisoner. If the town won't hire Billy Wade, then I'll see that he's at least reimbursed by the federal government for his time."

Duncan nodded with distraction, his eyes now scanning the earth for another ant.

"So long," Longarm said, "and thanks for the big rifle."

Duncan looked up quickly. "So long, Marshal Long. Just bring everything back and I'll pay you fifty cents on the dollar, if you don't get yourself killed out there."

Longarm figured that made good sense. He rode up the street, feeling everyone's eyes boring into him. They would know that he was leaving, and then all hell would break loose again. During the last day or so, things had been noticeably tamer, and Longarm was sure it was due to his presence.

"So long, Marshal!"

Longarm waved at Pete, who was standing in front of his Wildcat Waterhole Saloon. "Thanks."

A few doors up the street, Billy stepped out of the marshal's office to meet Longarm. "Hell of a horse you got there, Marshal Long. A fine animal."

"Yes," Longarm said, "he is."

"Where'd you get that big rifle?"

"Borrowed it," Longarm said, noticing that Billy had polished York's badge to a shine and was wearing it on his chest. "You going to be all right?"

''Yes, sir! I can take care of myself and your prisoner. Don't you worry about me. Just bring those three bank robbers back—dead or alive.''

''I will,'' Longarm vowed. He lowered his voice and said, ''After I leave, I'm almost certain that the rough element in this town will test you, Billy.''

''I know that,'' he replied, not sounding a bit worried. ''I've thought it out and I'm prepared to take control.''

''No second thoughts?''

''Not a one, Marshal. I can handle this town.''

Longarm had his doubts, but there was no sense in voicing them. He needed to get going, and he sure couldn't take Ike Moffit with him. ''Good luck. I should be back within a few weeks.''

''We'll be fine,'' Billy promised. ''And I'll keep an eye on Mrs. York for you.''

Longarm paused, then managed to say, ''You do that.''

He rode to the edge of town, nodding this way and that at the few law-abiding citizens who probably regretted his leaving and had come out to wish him farewell. When Longarm reined the mustang up before Donita's house, she was sitting in her late husband's rocking chair and looked depressed.

''It's going to work out just fine,'' Longarm said, not trusting himself to dismount and kiss her good-bye. ''I swear that I'll come back and take you to Denver, if you still have a mind to leave Whiskey Creek.''

''I'll have a mind and I'll be packed,'' she told him, not leaving her chair. ''If I have to sell this house for a dollar, then that's exactly what I'll do.''

''Sure,'' he said, also feeling kind of low.

''Custis?''

''Yeah.''

Donita took a deep breath. ''It'd just break my heart if I lost two good lawmen. I hope you know that.''

''I know it.''

Longarm tipped his hat to Donita, and then he reined his roan mustang southeast and put it into a gallop that carried him out of Whiskey Creek and off toward the distant Ruby Mountains.

Two hours later, Marshal Billy Wade sealed a letter and walked over to the stage station, where a coach was about to depart. "I need to post this letter to the marshal's office in Elko before he leaves to come pay us a visit."

Andy, the same driver that had brought Longarm into town, gazed down at the young man. "You gonna try and be the law here?"

"I'm going to do a hell of a lot more than try." Billy touched his badge. "And driver, I'd appreciate it if you'd refer to me as Marshal Wade the next time we speak. Is that clearly understood?"

The driver blushed with anger, but he nodded his head and grunted, "Yep."

"Yep, what?"

The driver swallowed. "Yep, Marshal Wade."

Wade relaxed. "Good. You learn fast. Now make sure this letter gets to the marshal in Elko. We don't need him nosin' around in our neighborhood. He's got trouble enough taking care of things in his own town."

"Yes, sir."

A few minutes later, the stagecoach rolled out and Billy Wade smiled, then headed down the street ignoring the drunkenness and debauchery that had taken hold of Whiskey Creek again. His youthful face was serene, and he looked happy when he arrived at Donita York's house and knocked on her front door.

There was no answer, so he stepped inside. It was cool and dim, and Billy could smell Donita's lilac perfume as he tiptoed softly down the hall, He paused at her bedroom door and peered inside. It was empty, but he went in anyway. He removed his hat, then stretched out on the top of her bed, plenty happy to wait for her return.

An hour passed before Wade heard the front door open with a squeak. He smiled and sat up, then tiptoed over to hide behind the bedroom door. He listened to Donita as she moved around in the kitchen, and when he heard her hum a tune, he smiled even more.

Donita finally walked past Billy to her bed. Billy shut the bedroom door and said in his most cheerful voice, "Hello, pretty woman. I'm your next lawman."

Donita whirled, black eyes flashing. "Who are you? Get out of my house!"

"Uh-uh," he said, tapping his badge. "Marshal Long took your husband's place. Now he's gone and I'm taking his place."

"Get out!"

Billy took a step closer to her. "You're a handsome wench. I like your fire too."

Donita kept a derringer in her bedside drawer, and now she lunged for it. Too late Billy saw his mistake in not moving around the bed so that he could reach her quickly. The derringer came up and Billy's own hand flashed for his six-gun.

"Mexican standoff," he said, cocking back the hammer of his Colt. "If you don't shoot me, I won't shoot you. Fair enough, honey?"

"If you ever set foot on my property again, I'll kill you! Do you understand, Señor?"

Billy discovered that his throat was suddenly very dry and he wanted a drink. "Yeah, I understand that you love men who wear badges. I'm wearing a badge and I'm going to have you because it's my turn."

"It's your turn to die if you try to touch me."

Billy realized that the woman was not bluffing. He didn't understand this, but he decided he had better leave. "We'll try this again soon when you haven't had a man for a few days. You look like the kind of woman who can't live without it more than forty-eight hours. I'll be back."

The derringer in her fist shivered. Billy laughed and holstered his gun.

"Adios, Señorita," he said, tipping his hat in farewell. "And don't worry, you're going to like me better than either one of the other two you had. We're going to have a whole lot of fun as soon as I get this town straightened out."

"Out!"

Billy was not accustomed to being rebuffed by women. Almost always, his conquests had been quick and pleasurable. He considered himself an accomplished lover as well as a shootist. Donita York, he decided, simply did not know what she was missing, but he could change that in a hurry.

"Oh, by the way," Billy said before stepping through the front door, "I'll be by with some laundry for you to wash."

"I'll throw it in the dirt!"

"If you do that," he said with a cold grin, "I'll make you crawl around and pick it up with your cock-sucking lips."

Donita raised her derringer and fired, but Billy was already out the door and running toward the street, laughing like crazy. He had seen the shock and outrage on the Widow York's pretty face, and knew he'd hurt her bad. Later, he'd turn things around and treat her like a damned queen. Then he'd have her licking out of the palm of his hand like a puppy dog.

Billy looked back at Donita's house, hoping to see her once again, but she was still inside. No matter. Business before pleasure, and the first order of business was to form up a town council and get appointed as their marshal. After that, he would put the bad element of Whiskey Creek on notice that they would have to park their guns at his office when they arrived in town. A few would object, of course, but after he shot one or two, the rest would fall in line.

Just as they had before.

Chapter 8

Billy Wade went to the printer, Isaac Bean, who published the weekly *Whiskey Creek Gazette,* and said, "I want you to print a flyer for me."

"Who's payin' for it?"

Billy thought a few moments and then he said, "The city, I guess."

"What city!"

"The city that will be formed after the town council is elected."

"The what?" Bean was clearly confused.

"And I want you to be on it," Billy decided. "You look like a man that ought to serve his community."

Isaac's hands were black from printer's ink, and his shoulders were humped from too many long hours of slaving over tintype and his broken-down Washington Printing Press.

"Mister, I can see the badge that you're wearing, but anyone can pin on a badge. Now just who are you?"

"I'm Marshal Billy Wade and I'm going to set about cleaning up this shit-house of a town. We're going to make it law-abiding and God-fearing."

"Whiskey Creek?" The old man threw back his head and laughed. "Mister," he said when he could speak again, "you don't look drunk, but you sure as hell can't be sober either. There ain't no city council and there never will be. This is just a wide-open sonofabitch and that's how it'll stay."

"Wrong," Billy said, reaching for a pad of paper. "Now here's what I want you to put on the flyers. Print about a hundred and hire some kid to tack the sonsabitches up on every porch post, tree, and shitter in town."

But Isaac shook his head and folded his still-powerful arms across the front of his ink-stained apron. "Uh-uh," he said, jaw jutting out defiantly. "Mister, we've both had our little laugh for the day and now it's time that I got back to work. So skedaddle unless you got some *real* news for next week's edition."

Billy leaned forward and said, "Listen, you stupid old man. I'm the new marshal of Whiskey Creek and I'm forming a town council. They're going to officially appoint me your marshal and maybe, if you support me, I'll decide to make sure that you're appointed mayor."

"I wouldn't be mayor of Whiskey Creek for love nor gold!"

"Then the hell with you," Billy swore, penning his flyer's message with a large and ornate scrawl. "Just print a hundred of these and make sure they are posted on the street by tomorrow morning."

Isaac came over and studied the message. "I'll be damned if I will," he said after reading it in a glance.

Billy drew his six-gun, cocked it, and placed the barrel to rest between the printer's bulging eyes. "And you'll be dead if you don't."

A bead of sweat burst across Isaac's brow, and his eyes widened with fear. "All right," he breathed. "A hundred will be out by tomorrow morning."

"Good," Billy said. "And if they aren't, I'll just have to arrest you."

"On what charges?"

"I don't know," Billy said with a malicious grin, "but I'd sure as hell think of something. And if you tried to escape . . . well, that could be fatal."

Isaac wiped his brow. "Yeah," he said as Billy turned to go, "I expect it might be. Who else are you going to insist be on your self-appointed city council?"

"I don't know," Billy said with an amiable shrug, "whoever wins tomorrow afternoon's election."

"Marshal, do you really believe that you'll live to pull this off?"

"I do." Billy turned to leave, and then he stopped. "By the way, who is the top dog in Whiskey Creek?"

"Huh?"

"You heard me. Every town has got at least one man that calls the shots. Someone who has risen out of the gutter and cracks the whip over the other slime. Someone who gets others to do his dirty work. Who is that man in Whiskey Creek?"

"I don't know."

"Yes, you do," Billy replied, coming back over to stand before him. "You damn sure do. I can find out soon enough, but why don't you just save me the trouble? Who is it?"

Isaac gulped and removed his wire-rimmed glasses because he was sweating and blurring the lenses. He wiped the glasses off and replaced them.

"Come on! Come on!" Billy said impatiently.

"Uh, all right. If I was to choose one man who sort of pulled the strings, it would be Alf Tucker."

"Alf Tucker? Who the hell is he, a saloon owner?"

"Alf owns a couple of saloons, but mostly he just invests and keeps his finger in things. Alf owns a piece of most everything in Whiskey Creek."

"Where does he live?"

"He has a big ranch about four miles northeast of here, but he mostly stays in town."

"Is he a family man, or a womanizer?"

"Alf's wife died about three years ago. He has a no-account son that lives in Reno and a daughter that is going to some fancy Eastern college."

"So he lives alone?"

"Sometimes. Alf has a girlfriend."

"Who?"

Isaac looked pained. "I don't know why you don't just ask someone else. Everything I'm telling you is common knowledge."

"Then it shouldn't bother you to tell me."

"All right. Alf's woman is named Rose. She runs the Bearclaw Bar, which Alf just happens to own. She looks over some of the girls that work there and she even tends the bar. But mostly, she tends to Alf."

"I see." Billy's brow knitted. "What about protection?"

"Protection?"

"Yeah. A man as wealthy and powerful as Alf Tucker is bound to have enemies, so he'll hire a little protection. Maybe a couple of hired guns and a bully or two."

"Not Alf."

"Where's his office?"

"At the only bank we have in the town, and they're crooked as snakes. They're charging a man an arm and a leg to borrow money. Interest rates are. . . ."

But Billy didn't hear what the interest rates were because he wasn't listening. He was going out the door, heading for the bank, which he recalled seeing just up the street. It was solid rock and rather imposing-looking, like a bank ought to look.

When he stepped into the bank, a teller about Billy's own age looked up from behind his cage and smiled. "Can I help you today, sir?"

"Yes, I'd like to see Mr. Tucker."

"Is he expecting you?"

"No, but he'll want to hear what I have to say."

The young teller tried to smile without much success. "And who shall I say is calling?"

"Tell him my name is Marshal Billy Wade and I'm here to make his acquaintance."

"Marshal Wade?" the teller repeated, obviously unsure that he had heard correctly.

"That's right."

"Just a moment, Marshal," the teller said as he twisted around toward a glass-enclosed office. "Oh, I'm afraid that Mr. Tucker is conferring with an associate right now. Would you have a seat in the lobby?"

"I don't believe I will," Billy said, spying a swinging door and heading for the banker's office.

"Hey! You can't come back here!"

"Sure I can," Billy called. "I'm your marshal and I can do about any damned thing that I want."

The teller actually tried to grab Billy's arm and stop him from bursting into Tucker's office. Billy unleashed a wicked backhand that broke the teller's lips. The man cried out in pain and covered his ashen face.

"You should never try to interfere with the law," Billy lectured sternly as he grabbed the knob on the door to Tucker's office. "You can get hurt very, very badly that way. In fact, you're real lucky that I didn't just break your nose."

The teller's eyes were misty with pain as Billy stepped into Tucker's office.

"Who the hell are you?" a big, fat man challenged, coming out of his chair behind a desk. "Who invited you in here without my permission?"

"Your little teller out there," Billy said, glancing at the other man in the room, who looked like a prosperous cattle rancher in his high-heeled boots and tailored suit. Neither man, Billy noted, was packing a side arm, although he suspected that they were both carrying concealed weapons.

"Who the hell are you?" Tucker asked again.

Billy pointed to his shiny badge. "As you can see, I'm your new marshal, and I was told that you are Whiskey Creek's most prosperous citizen."

"I don't think you're the marshal at all," Tucker said, not taking the bait of flattery. "And I think you had better get your ass out of my office before—"

"Before what? You call the law?"

The rancher came to his feet. He was about fifty, square-jawed, and rugged-looking, with a knife scar from some long-past fight. He had broad shoulders and looked tough and strong. "I think you'd better leave before I throw you out."

"I'm not leaving until I've had my say," Billy told them both. "And who are you?"

"Henry Judson, but—"

"Would you and your friend like to be on the new Whiskey Creek City Council that is being elected tomorrow?"

"Huh?"

"There will be an election and I've already appointed your printer. I'd like to have you especially, Mr. Tucker. But you look pretty good too, Mr. Judson. What do you say?"

Tucker and Judson exchanged glances, and the big rancher suddenly pivoted and unleashed a wicked uppercut that came almost from the floor. Billy was already moving sideways. When Judson's fist whistled past, Billy ducked under the rancher's arm and pounded the rancher twice in the gut. Judson grunted, but he was a hard man, and it wasn't until Billy's fist found the rancher's throat that the fight was over. Judson crumpled to his knees and Billy smashed him behind the ear, driving him to the floor.

"Hold it!" Billy shouted at the banker as his gun streaked up to line on the fat man's chest. "You're too rich to die a fool, Mr. Tucker, so ease back down in that big chair of yours and hear me out."

"You're a dead man," Tucker said without passion. "I'll see that you not only die, but die slowly."

"That would be a fatal mistake on your part," Billy said, trying to ignore the difficulty that the rancher was having getting his breath through a smashed throat. "And there's no need for us to be enemies. In fact, I'd like to become friends . . . and business partners."

"You're insane!"

"Nope. I've been appointed as a federal marshal in charge of this town and I do mean to start making some protection money off its businesses."

Billy smiled. "And I guess you own a whole lot of the businesses in this town, Mr. Tucker. So like it or not, we're going to become partners. I'm going to protect your business interests in Whiskey Creek, and in return, you'll see that I'm amply rewarded."

"Get out of my office."

Billy shrugged. "Sure. But I'll expect you to accept the nomination for city council. I've got the authority from a federal marshal right now, but I'd also like to have some local support too."

"Get out!"

"Sure. I realize this is all happening sort of sudden-like for you, Mr. Tucker. So it's just natural that you'd be thrown a little off balance. But once you've had time to sort of get used to the idea, I think you'll warm to it. And if not, well, then I'll just have to kill you in the line of duty."

Tucker leaned over his desk. He weighed at least three hundred pounds and was probably in his early fifties. His face was florid with liver spots and his jowls sagged heavily. He looked awful for a rich man, and Billy could not help but think that Tucker would not live to be an old man. He was soft and corrupt and only his eyes were still fierce and frightening.

Billy backed out of the office. "Your friend will recover,

although he might not be in good voice for a couple of days. I could have fixed it so that he'd never speak again, but I decided to be merciful."

"You are a dead man!"

"Yeah, I heard you say that before," Billy said. "But I'll tell you one thing, fat man. I'll take you with me if you send guns to bring me down. So tell them they had better not miss the first time because after I finish with 'em, you'll be next."

Tucker blanched and then his face turned bright red with rage.

"You'd better sit down before you have a heart seizure," Billy advised a moment before he left. "You look like you could croak any minute."

"Get . . . out!"

Billy nodded and backed out. Henry Judson was starting to get his color back, and he looked like a man who would go crazy once he was back on his feet.

"See you tomorrow, Councilmen!" Billy called as he headed for the front door.

Chapter 9

Billy knew that all hell was going to break loose and that he had just, as his granddaddy had been fond of saying, "tweaked the tail of the tiger." There was no doubt that Alf Tucker and Henry Judson were tough and determined men who would now set about to destroy him. The only real question was: how? If Billy had been just an ordinary cowboy when he'd pulled that audacious stunt back in Tucker's office, he'd probably have already been shot from ambush. But he had made it very clear that he was an appointed *federal* marshal, and that would keep Tucker and Judson guessing. It was one thing to shoot down a local-yokel lawman, quite another to kill a fed.

So what would those two rich and roughshod bastards do to him? This was the question that Billy asked himself as he strolled down Whiskey Creek's main street, looking as if he did not have a single care in the world. Before he reached the Bearclaw Bar, Billy decided that the thing to do was to take the offensive and provoke Tucker and Judson even more. What was absolutely essential, Billy was quite sure, was to push them into some kind of immediate confrontation.

With that decided, Billy waltzed into the Bearclaw Saloon looking for Alf Tucker's woman, the one that they called Rose.

The Bearclaw was a cut above most mining town saloons and quite popular, judging from the number of miners in attendance. There was a real bar instead of the usual two or three planks stretched across whiskey barrels. It was made of mahogany and hand-carved, with brass foot rails and matching spittoons. There were four or five poker and faro tables and all of them were occupied.

"What'll you have, mister?" the bartender asked with a tired smile.

"I'd like a sarsaparilla."

"A sarsaparilla?"

"Yes. Cherry-flavored, if you have it."

The bartender heaved a deep sigh. "I have root beer and there's coffee brewing in the back room. Or maybe you'd like a glass of cool goat's milk."

"The root beer will be fine," Billy said. "Oh, yes, and I'd like to see Rose."

The bartender had been reaching for the root beer, but now he paused. "What for?"

Billy removed the marshal's badge from his shirt pocket and laid it on the mahogany bar. "Tell her that Marshal Billy Wade has come to pay his respects."

"She's still asleep," the bartender said after a long look at the badge. He motioned over his shoulder. "Miss Rose works nights and sleeps until about six in the afternoon. But I'll tell her—"

"Show me to her room," Billy ordered with an edge of authority now in his voice.

The bartender was middle-aged, slight of build, and he wore a scraggly black goatee and mustache. "I can't do that," he tried to explain. "You see, I work for Miss Rose and she requires her beauty sleep."

"Well," Billy said, starting around the bar toward a back

door. "I think that she'll just have to do without her 'beauty sleep' this morning."

"Hey, stop!"

But Billy kept on moving. He passed through the door and entered a dim and narrow hallway with small rooms or cribs lining both sides. He started to grab the first doorknob he could reach, but the bartender objected, saying, "That's not Miss Rose's room!"

"Then which one is it?"

"Last door on the right," the bartender snapped, "but for gawdsakes don't let her know that I told you so."

Billy marched down the hallway and knocked on Rose's door. When there was no answer he tried the knob, but the door was locked.

"Miss Rose!" he called, banging her door hard with his fists. "Miss Rose, it's Marshal Billy Wade come a-callin'. Please open up!"

"Go away!" Rose shouted, her voice slightly drugged by sleep and whatever she had consumed the night before. "Go away!"

But Billy had other plans. He reared back and kicked the door open. The bartender's jaw dropped, and then he wheeled and disappeared, probably to get Alf Tucker or someone else to come and help.

Billy stepped into the room, half expecting to see an aging, whiskey-soaked whore. Instead, he saw a woman who did show some years, but was still very attractive. Billy guessed that she was maybe ten years older than himself, but that didn't bother him a whit. Rose was a big, buxom redheaded woman, and she was wearing a green silk nightgown that was most revealing.

"Are you crazy?" she shouted. "Get out of here!"

Billy laughed and walked over to the woman's bed. He smiled and stuck out his hand. "I'm your new marshal. Name is Billy Wade and I've been appointed by United States Deputy Marshal Custis Long to clean up this miserable town.

Just thought that you ought to know, Miss Rose."

"You must be drunk!"

Billy laughed and sat down beside her. When she reached for a derringer under her pillow, Billy easily grabbed the weapon and stuffed it into his waistband.

Rose was furious. Her green eyes matched the color of her nightgown and they glittered with hatred. "You're going to pay for this!"

"Then I might just as well enjoy myself," was Billy's casual response as his hand reached under the covers and began to explore the woman's voluptuous body.

When Rose tried to rake his face with her fingernails, Billy slapped her hard and then he kissed her mouth. Rose struggled, and that made him more excited. His finger found the honey pot between her thighs and entered her warm wetness. Rose cursed and struggled, but Billy sensed that her heart was not really in the fight. He was seriously debating whether or not to tear off his clothing and mount Rose—broken door be damned—when he heard a shout up the hall and then the pounding of boots.

Billy yanked his trigger finger out of Rose and wiped it dry on his pants. "I met Alf a little while ago," he said, drawing his gun. "And while I admit that the old bastard has a lot of money, I've got what you *really* want."

"You're an insufferable bastard, aren't you?" she said, large and sagging breasts heaving. "Too bad you've got about fifteen seconds left to live."

"Don't count on that," Billy told her. "And if you're smart, you'll get your sweet ass off that bed quick because the bullets are going to start flying."

Rose might have been mad and she might have been sexually aroused, but she was also smart. She rolled sideways and went right off the bed, striking the floor. Billy wasn't watching, however, as he dropped to the floor himself, extended his six-gun out before him, and cocked back the hammer.

The first of Alf Tucker's gunmen foolishly filled the doorway. Billy shot him cleanly through the chest and he crashed over backward, twitching and bleeding in the hallway. Billy waited a moment, then fired two more bullets, each spaced about a foot out from the sides of the door frame. He heard a cry of pain and grinned as the steps retreated.

There was a lot of confusion going on in the hallway. Billy could hear shouts and the sound of more men running. He sleeved the sweat from his forehead and glanced back over his shoulder.

Rose had inched up from the floor and was watching him. "You're finished," she said. "You'll never get out of this alive."

"I'm a federal marshal," Billy replied, "and these dumb bastards need to understand what that means."

"They don't need to understand anything," Rose said, looking pleased that he was about to be killed.

Billy inhaled deeply and reminded himself that he'd asked for this quick and dramatic confrontation. And Rose was correct about one thing—he could not kill everyone. That meant that his only hope was probably bravado rather than bullets.

"I'm a federal marshal!" he shouted into the hallway. "And I'm coming out. The first man that tries to kill me will either be shot or hanged by the United States Army!"

Billy added the last part about the army because he remembered there was an army outpost somewhere in northern Nevada.

"Drop your guns and come forward!" he called.

Billy listened, but there was no sound of guns being dropped to the hallway floor.

"A dead man for sure," Rose snickered.

"Shut up," Billy ordered before he shouted through the open doorway, "I'm coming out and I'll shoot or arrest anyone who tries to interfere with the law!"

Billy quickly reloaded his gun and then he spun the cylinder. He impulsively blew Rose a kiss. "We're not finished with what I just got started."

Instead of cutting him with an unkind word as Billy expected, Rose said, "I'll give you this much, you got a big set of brass balls."

"Wait'll you take a gander at what comes attached to 'em," Billy told her as he cocked both his six-gun and Rose's derringer and stepped out into the hallway.

Only two professional gunmen were waiting, and Billy dropped to his knees with his six-gun and that two-shot derringer barking very much like a big dog and a little terrier. In return, a bullet nicked his ear, two more parted his hair and creased his scalp. But before the gunmen could react and lower their sights, they were both dancing with the devil. Billy's shots kicked them backward, goose-stepping like martinets. He shot maybe six rounds between the two pistols, and figured he only missed once, and that was with the second bullet out of the derringer. The two men died on their feet, and when they hit the floor they didn't even quiver.

The smoke and the din of the battle filled his ears and his nostrils, and Billy came erect. He backed through the doorway and pitched Rose her empty derringer as he quickly reloaded his six-gun.

Rose didn't say a word, but just stared at him.

Billy finished reloading, and then he turned his attention back to her. "The undertaker is going to be a busy man today. I put down three. How many more do you expect Alf will send?"

"As many as it takes."

"I was afraid of that," Billy said. "I guess that he'll just have to be convinced that I'll kill him next if he sends anyone else at me."

"Who are you?"

"I'm the man that's going to take Alf's place in this town and in your bed."

Rose bit her lower lip and her chin dipped with acceptance of this fact, causing Billy to smile. "See you later tonight."

"I can't see you! I'm Alf's woman."

"Not anymore you're not."

"The hell you say! He pays the bills, buster. You may be good with a gun, but that won't buy me what I need."

"Patience, woman," he said. "Before you know it, I'll have enough money to meet your every desire."

"Talk comes cheap."

"I can back mine up," he told her. "The proof is lying out in the hallway if you care to take a look."

Rose shook her head, then said, "Don't come around before midnight—if you're still alive. And come in through the back-alley door."

"You still don't have much faith in me, do you, Rose?"

"Why should I? Gunfighters come cheap."

"I'm a federal marshal."

"You're a gunfighter. Maybe the best I've ever seen, but a gunfighter all the same."

Billy saw there was no use arguing with the woman. Tonight, when he returned, he show her that he was a whole lot more than a gunfighter. He'd show her he was a real stud.

When Billy stepped outside, the hallway was completely deserted except for the three bodies. Billy grabbed the last one and dragged the corpse back through the door and out to the bar. There were men crowded around, but when they saw Billy with a smoking six-gun in one fist and the dead man in the other, they retreated in fear.

"I'm Federal Marshal Billy Wade," he announced to everyone. "And I mean to announce a rule that every man will check his gun in at my office when he comes into town and he'll get it back when he leaves."

The men, almost all of whom were miners, looked astonished. One of them dared to blurt out, "But this is Whiskey Creek!"

"That's right, but it's going to be a *different* Whiskey Creek. One where men aren't killing each other every night."

A heavyset man in bib overalls and no shirt but with a pair of work boots pushed forward to ask, "And you're going to do this all by yourself?"

"No," Billy said. "As a matter of fact, I'm calling for an election tomorrow."

"An election?"

"That's right. Would any of you gentlemen care to run for mayor or the city council?"

The miners exchanged confused glances. No one said a word.

"No matter," Billy told them. "I'll find some candidates. Just remove your weapons and go back to your fun."

"What about knives?" one of them asked.

"You can keep your knives, but if you stab someone to death, you'll be hanged within twenty-four hours. And if you just cut them, you'll suffer the consequences."

The miners were a rough-looking bunch, and there were a few that were trying to muster up the courage to challenge Billy until he said, "There are two more dead men in the hall. Someone drag them out here and someone else go fetch the undertaker. The rest of you, just shuck your guns."

Billy was not surprised when first one miner and then all the rest of them disarmed themselves. Most men, Billy had discovered, were really very little more than complicated sheep. He figured it was human nature for ignorant men to do what everyone else did, especially when that kept you for being singled out for punishment.

"You, you, and you," Billy said, pointing, "collect

those guns and bring them over to my office and dump them in the middle of the floor.''

''What are you going to do now?''

''Why,'' Billy said, ''I'm going to collect every gun I see in Whiskey Creek and add them to the collection. What the hell did you think?''

The miners looked confused, which only told Billy that the ability to think was not their greatest attribute. They were, by and large, rough, dirty, and brutish men because it took that breed to survive in the dangerous and back-breaking bowels of a mine.

Chapter 10

Alf Tucker closed his bank early that day, and sent out word that he would pay five hundred dollars to the man who gunned down Marshal Billy Wade.

"Those were three pretty good men that he dropped at the Bearclaw," Judson breathed, his voice still little more than a dry whisper. "This young federal marshal must be one hell of a gunslinger."

"Or he's just plain lucky," Tucker said, jamming a cigar into his mouth. "Don't matter, though, because his luck is just about to run out."

"I hear he's disarming the whole damned town," Judson croaked. "Two men tried to shoot him in one of the saloons, but Marshal Wade got the drop on them both and they're in jail. I think we're going to have to face up to the fact that he's a federal law officer."

"He's a *dead* federal officer," Tucker spat. "And, if I could find out who told him that Rose is my woman, that man would be dead too."

"Why don't we all just get our guns out, march over there to his office, and blow Wade to hell?"

"Because we'd be the first ones that he dropped," Tucker said with a tone of disgust. "The right way to kill that sonofabitch is just to put up the bounty and let whoever has the guts to try for it figure the best way to bushwhack our new federal marshal.''

''I'd sure like to have another try at him,'' Judson said, his voice choking with anger.

''I think we'd both better just step aside on this one,'' Tucker advised. ''We got a man here who is as dangerous as a rattlesnake and who obviously won't kill easy.''

''With a five-hundred-dollar reward on his head, someone is bound to get him,'' Judson said confidently. ''He won't last out the night. Did he touch Rose?''

''No,'' Tucker said quickly. ''She said he looked like he wanted to, but the fighting started too soon.''

''Damn good thing.''

''Yeah. I'm going back over to see Rose now. She's upset, but she'll feel better knowing that I'm putting that bounty on the marshal.''

''Maybe you should move her.''

''Move her?''

''Sure. Put her up someplace else until this Wade fella is dead.''

''Not necessary,'' Tucker growled, reaching for his coat. A few moments later, he and Judson were walking down the street, nodding grimly to the people of Whiskey Creek.

''Is it true that you're offering five hundred dollars for the first one that puts a bullet in that new marshal?'' a man asked.

''That's right,'' Tucker snapped, answering that same question for perhaps the twentieth time since leaving the office. ''So why don't you get a six-gun and be the lucky one to collect?''

''Not me,'' the man replied with a shake of his head. ''I heard what he did to those three gunslingers over at the Bearclaw. If they couldn't kill him, how the hell could I?''

''Someone is going to do it, why not you?''

''Because a dead man can't spend money,'' the man said, walking away.

Both Tucker and Judson paused across the street from the marshal's office. It was a warm afternoon and the marshal's door was wide open to catch a breeze.

"Bold bastard, ain't he," Judson wheezed. "It'll be good to see him stretched out on a board with about fifty bullet holes in his carcass."

"Yeah," Tucker said, waddling on toward the Bearclaw, "it sure as hell will!"

When Tucker opened Rose's door, she was lying on her bed, just staring up at the ceiling. He removed his hat and went over to her bedside. He felt a stirring in his groin and he laid his liver spotted hand on her breast, but she batted it away.

"I'm not in the mood, Alf. Not after this morning."

"That's done," he said, trying to keep from losing his temper. "And I've offered a five-hundred-dollar reward to the first man who puts a bullet in Marshal Wade."

Rose's eyes widened, and she scooted up against her headboard. "Five hundred, huh?"

"Yeah. And there are plenty of men who are willing to try for it. Wade will be a dead man just as soon as he steps outside that office."

"But won't it go hard on you when the feds learn that you put a bounty on a federal marshal?"

"I'll worry about that later. First we kill the serpent, then we bury and forget it."

"I see."

Alf placed his hand back over one of Rose's large breasts and said, "Are you hungry, darling?"

"No." She reached for her whiskey. "I'm just thirsty."

He studied her with disapproval. "You shouldn't take this thing so hard. The sonofabitch got lucky and now he's about to get shot. That's all."

"Sure."

"You sure that he didn't do anything to you, Rose?"

"Of course not! You must have heard everyone tell you

that he was only in here about two minutes before those three gunmen arrived and we had a full-scale shootout in the hallway. How much do you think he could have done in two minutes?''

Before Tucker could reply, Rose smiled. ''Well, considering that you do it in under two minutes, I guess I can understand your question.''

Tucker's already florid cheeks turned pink. ''You have a sharp and cutting tongue. Rose. And someday, I'm going to have to punish you for the use of it.''

''Don't try and scare me,'' Rose said, her voice hard and flat. ''I may be young enough to be your daughter, but I'm not and I've had about all the shit from men that I'm willing to take in one day.''

Tucker got up. ''Then why don't you just drink yourself into a stupor and take a fresh look at things in the morning? Marshal Wade will probably be on display tomorrow before we toss him into a shallow grave.''

''Where are you going?''

''To eat.''

Rose's lips curled downward with contempt. ''Might do you good to miss a meal or two, Alf. Might do you a lot of good.''

''Like I said, you got a sharp and a cutting tongue. And I don't forget an insult. Sooner or later, it's going to catch up with you.''

''I'm scared,'' she said mockingly, tossing down her drink. ''Real, real scared.''

''I may be back after supper,'' Tucker announced. ''And you know what I'll want.''

''You can want all you want, but that don't mean you'll get it from me.''

''Imagine working the cribs again, Rose,'' Tucker said, his voice cold with pent-up fury. ''Think real hard about screwing a dozen unwashed miners every day and half the night. Just like you were doing before I made life easy for you."

The thought was so abhorrent that it caused Rose to drink straight from the bottle.

Seeing her pale, Tucker chuckled. "I'll be back, Rose. And I'll expect my usual pleasures."

Tucker made a hurried exit and Rose kept on drinking. It almost seemed as if everything that had transpired this morning was a dream. Had a handsome young man really come to her bed and diddled her with his finger, then shot three of Alf's best gunnies? Rose took a drink and shook her head. If it was all a dream, she wondered if it would reappear at midnight as promised.

There was nothing to do but to drink and wait and see.

Chapter 11

Rose knew she was already drunk by the time Alf returned to her room after supper. And when she saw his flushed face and bloodshot eyes, she knew that Alf was a little drunk himself.

"Did you bring a fresh bottle?" she asked as he closed and locked her door.

Alf wheeled around, almost losing his balance. "Don't I always?"

"Let's not stand on formalities." Rose said, pushing herself up in her bed and motioning Alf to come forward. "First the bottle, then the two-minute fuck."

Alf's mouth pinched down at the corner. "You're a beautiful woman, but you have a foul mouth. I wish you weren't so damned coarse."

"I'm a whore, for crissakes!"

"You're my woman!"

Rose almost corrected the man, but she was just sober enough to realize that would be a mistake. When sober, Alf could be insulted and even humiliated, but when drunk, he could get mean. He might even attack her, although Rose was quite sure that she could physically hold her own against him.

"Here," he said, pulling a pint bottle out of his coat

pocket and beginning to undress. "I don't want to argue with you tonight, Rose. It's been a bad day."

"Because of this Marshal Wade?"

"Yeah. But that little problem is about to be solved." Tucker's lips pulled back with satisfaction. "Because of that five-hundred-dollar bounty, Wade hasn't a chance."

Rose uncorked the bottle. She knew that what Alf said was no doubt the truth, but she didn't want to admit the fact. She inspected the bottle, her lips turning down with disapproval. "Only a pint?"

"I think we've both already had more than enough to drink," he grunted, collapsing on the bed and trying to reach down and untie his shoelaces.

The sight of Alf without clothes was pretty repulsive, and Rose turned toward the window, uncorking the bottle and drinking the liquor in deep, noisy gulps.

"Maybe you better slow down on that," Alf said, standing up to unbutton his shirt and remove his baggy trousers.

"I will if you turn off the light so I don't have to see you in the naked flesh."

He flushed with embarrassment, and even tried to suck in his huge gut. "You bitch!"

Rose giggled and drank some more. She closed her eyes and listened to Alf as he grunted, probably trying to reach over and pull off his stockings. Normally she did that, and whatever else Alf wanted while she was on her knees but not tonight.

"Turn out the lamp on your side of the bed," she ordered, blowing out her own bedside lamp.

"No," he snarled. "Tonight, by gawd, I'm going to get an eyeful just because you've already given me a bellyful of your insults."

Rose turned to look at him, and he ripped the bottle from her hand and slammed it down on his bedside table. He was huge-bellied, and his chest was matted with gray hair, as was his crotch. Despite being numb with drink,

Rose felt awash with revulsion and she started to turn away, but he grabbed her thighs and drove himself into her body.

"Take it easy!" she cried, recoiling with pain. "Alf, you're crushing and hurting me! Let me get on top the way we usually do!"

"No. Maybe you need to be crushed and hurt," he grunted as he began to rut furiously despite the fact that she was very dry. It seemed to Rose that he was tearing her up inside.

Rose struggled, but his weight was too much to budge, so she lay still and clenched her teeth until her juices made the union slick and bearable.

"Come on, whore!" he panted, his swollen body pounding the breath out of her. "You've been paid, now perform!"

"I hate you!" Rose cried, reaching around and grabbing his flabby buttocks and deciding to make him come as quickly as possible in order to get through this punishment.

It did not take her long because she knew how to use her body to bring a man to a climax. In just a few minutes his fat ass was jerking up and down like the butt of a buck rabbit when it coupled.

Rose pushed him off and looked over at him, her eyes burning with hatred. She saw that he was sweating and wheezing, and then he began to cough.

"I expect that, one of these days, I'll probably fuck you to death, Alf."

"I hope so," he muttered, reaching for the whiskey that still remained in their pint bottle. "I certainly hope so."

Rose took the bottle from him and drained the last of it before she rolled over, feeling his seed leaking out of her body and messing up the expensive silk sheets Alf had given her. She forced her thighs tightly together in order to expel as much of him as she could, and then she belched and began to think about the handsome Marshal Wade and his young, hard body. And just thinking about what he'd already done to her with just his finger, and what he'd promised to do tonight, made her cheeks burn and her nipples harden.

Rose heard Alf began to snore, and she tried to block out the sound. Be realistic, she told herself. Billy Wade was a dead man. It was crazy to expect that the marshal would be able to survive. But just in case, Rose eased out of bed, tiptoed to the door, and unlocked it.

If Billy was able to reach her door, Rose wanted him to come on inside and kill Alf Tucker.

Back at the marshal's office, Billy consulted his pocket watch. It was time to visit Rose. Time to slip out of this death trap.

Billy stood up and stretched, then picked up the jail cell keys. Ike Moffitt and his other two prisoners were snoring to the rafters. Billy went over and unlocked the door, knowing that he had to move fast.

"All right, boys, you're free. So get out of here before I change my mind!"

The prisoners roused. "What the hell time is it?" Ike muttered.

"Time to go," Billy repeated as he pushed Ike out of the cell and followed with the other two men. "Now hurry up and get out of here!"

They were too groggy to think about much except freedom, and when Billy propelled them outside, they didn't have a clue that at least four ambushers would open fire on them without warning. Billy ducked behind them and ran, keeping low and to the shadows as the night was shredded by frenzied gunfire. He heard screams and then the sound of bodies striking the boardwalk. But by then Billy was ducking around the corner and sprinting up a dark alley toward Rose's room and the many pleasures that awaited him.

When he reached her door a few minutes later and discovered that it was unlocked, Billy grinned hugely and let himself inside.

Rose was sitting up in bed with her lamp turned down low. Beside her lay Alf Tucker, looking like a bloated bull.

"Good evening, Rose!"

She shook her head as if she were seeing an illusion. "I thought that you were dead when I heard all that gunfire a few minutes ago."

"Not me," Billy said, closing the door and locking it. "But I'm convinced that there are a lot of folks out there who'd like to see me dead."

"So what happens now?"

He removed his gunbelt. "I think you know the answer to that."

"With *him* in my bed?" she asked, motioning toward the snoring Alf.

Billy chuckled. "I guess that bed would be a little crowded with the three of us. Maybe tonight we'll just spread a blanket on the floor and do some hard humpin', huh, darlin'?"

Rose didn't think twice about it. She climbed out of bed, almost lost her balance, and threw herself into Billy's arms. Her lips found his, and then he was pulling her down to the floor. Rose forgot all about the snoring Alf, and she gave herself to Billy more energetically than she'd given herself to any man during the last twenty years.

Their bodies seemed made for each other, and when their passion finally exploded, Rose could not stop quivering as wave after wave of pleasure threatened to consume her. Billy buried his face between her sweaty breasts, and it was a long time before either of them could even speak.

"You were wonderful," Rose finally panted. "I don't know what I'd do if you were to die."

"I'm not going to die," he promised, climbing off her and dressing quickly. "I'm going to get rich."

"How?"

Billy chuckled. "Alf is going to have a big change of heart tonight and decide to support me and my candidates for the city council."

"He is?" Rose was wishing she had not drunk so much whiskey because none of this made any sense.

"Yep. I'm going to wake him up and convince him right now. But I'd better tell you something first. I want you to pretend that nothing happened between us just now."

"Why?"

"Because I want him to think you're still his woman and that you're supporting him all the way."

"But I *hate* him!"

"I know," Billy said, buckling on his gunbelt and taking Rose in his arms. "But it's just better if he doesn't know that. You see, I'll need someone to keep an eye on him."

"No, Billy!" she pleaded.

His voice lost its warmth and his fingernails bit lightly into her flesh. "Rose, we're going to drain him of every dollar he owns, but we need to work together. And if he tries to double-cross me, which he probably will, I'll need some warning. Do you understand?"

She reluctantly nodded. "But when we've broken him, then what?"

"Then we take over his bank, the town, his ranch, and everything else. And we live happily ever after."

"Together, right?"

He kissed her long and passionately, and Rose felt like a schoolgirl again. Her heart fluttered when he said, "Sure, Rose. We'll even get married when the time is right. Would you like to do that?"

"More than anything!"

"All right," he said, looking deeply into her eyes. "Wake the fat man up and I'll convince him. It will help if you pretend to be a little frightened of me and protective of him."

"That won't be easy."

"Yes, it will," Billy said. "I got a hunch you've been fooling men for a lot of years."

Rose was a little offended and hurt by that statement. Did Billy mean that he thought her old? Or just coy and conniving? Before Rose could decide, Billy had his six-gun out and was jabbing it into Alf's side.

"Hey, wake up!"

Alf had always been a heavy sleeper, but he was jolted by the sharp pain in his side, and even Rose winced to see how hard Billy was sticking him with the barrel of that six-gun.

"Wake up, Mr. Tucker! Rise and shine!"

Alf grunted with pain and both his eyes and his mouth snapped open. "Uhh!" he gasped.

Billy scowled. "Come on, Mr. Tucker. Wake up because we've got some important matters to discuss."

Rose couldn't help herself, and began to giggle. "He doesn't look like he wants to talk very much."

"I hope he's soberer than you are," Billy said, going over to the bedside table and filling a glass of water. He went back to stand before Alf, and then he pitched the glassful of water into the banker's slack face. Alf choked and sputtered, but he woke up and started cursing.

Billy jammed his six-gun into Alf's solar plexus real hard, and Alf turned fish-belly white.

"Now," Billy said, "you're going to listen and I'm going to do the talking. Understand?"

It was all that Alf could do to nod his head. He was drooling, and he looked terrible enough that Rose almost felt sorry for the pig.

"All right," Billy said, pulling up a chair and straddling it backward. "Mr. Tucker, you are going to have a sudden and dramatic change of heart. You're going to get dressed and walk me outside and start telling everyone that you have decided to support me as the best choice for the marshal of Whiskey Creek. Then tomorrow, we'll have an election and I'll be in control."

Alf managed to shake his head. Billy jammed the barrel of his pistol a second time into Alf's gut, only this time it was even harder, and the front gunsight tore the flesh so that Alf began to bleed. When he saw his own blood, the last vestige of his resistance broke and he sobbed.

"No more! Please, no more!"

Rose smiled, but when Billy saw that, he shook his head and motioned for her to go to Alf.

Rose didn't want to, but she understood that this was her best chance to pretend loyalty. "You leave him be!" she cried, dropping to her knees before Alf. "Damn you, don't touch him again!"

Billy actually smiled. "All right, as long as he understands this new game and that I'll kill him *and* you if he doesn't cooperate."

"You . . ."

"Rose," Alf pleaded, "don't get into this. This is between the marshal and me."

"Please," she begged, "don't be so stubborn. Do whatever he says, Alf!"

"Okay," Alf choked. "You win, Marshal. What is it you want?"

Billy told him what he wanted in no uncertain terms. He wanted his candidates to win seats on the city council and he wanted Alf's unqualified endorsement. "And that old rancher friend of yours?"

"Henry Judson?"

"Yeah. Tell him to stay out of my sight or I'll break his neck the next time I see him. Got that?"

Alf was completely beaten. He sobbed and then nodded. "Anything else?"

"One last thing. Your businesses need protection and that's my specialty. That's why you're going to hire me."

Alf looked up. "But that's what a marshal is supposed to do anyway!"

"Yeah, well, I do a little extra. So I'll want . . . oh, two hundred dollars a month from you starting tomorrow."

"Two hundred dollars!"

"It's cheap," Billy explained. "After all, maybe somewhere out there lives another fighting sonofabitch almost as bad as me that I'll have to kill."

"Not very damned likely," Alf muttered.

"Mr. Tucker, you should clean yourself up and get dressed," Billy said, not bothering to hide his contempt. "You look awful."

"I feel awful."

"Rose, why don't you help him get dressed and cleaned up?" Billy suggested.

"Damn you, Marshal!" Rose cried, trying to muster up at least the semblance of passion. "I hate you for doing this!"

"Sure you do," Billy said with a wink of his eye. "But all that will change once you and Alf realize how safe I'm going to make Whiskey Creek. No more gunfights and knifings. Just law and order."

"You're not the law," Alf hissed. "You're just a—"

Before he could say anything more, Billy's hand shot out and he grabbed Alf by the throat and squeezed it until the older man's eyes bugged.

Letting go, he said, "What were you about to say, Mr. Tucker?"

A sob was torn from Alf and he shook his head, a beaten man. At that moment, Rose looked across at Billy and she felt a shiver of fear run through her.

And she needed another stiff drink.

Chapter 12

It was straight-up noon and the sun was an angry red blister when Longarm saw the buzzards circling over the rocky foothills. He had not heard any rifle fire, but from the number of birds of prey, he felt pretty sure that he would find something large and dead, maybe a man, but more likely a horse.

Longarm reined his gelding up into those hills, hat pulled down low to shield his face from the punishing sun. He let the roan mustang pick its own way up through the stunted sage and rocks, and the animal seemed to grew more excited the higher they climbed, probably because it had already traveled this very same trail.

The buzzards were circling over what seemed like a ridge until Longarm finally reached its crest, then looked down to see a steep wedge-shaped valley about two miles long and a quarter of a mile wide. There was a spring at the north end of the valley, marked by a couple of acres of dark green marsh grass. It would be the kind of oasis that mustangs would regularly seek in this hot arid country.

And that was what had gotten them killed. Longarm's features hardened as he counted seven dead mustangs, their black and bloated carcasses scattered across the valley. Longarm could see from the markings that the ones who had died near the spring had been dragged away from the precious water.

Suddenly, Longarm detected a movement in the brush. At that very same moment, Longarm's mustang caught the stench of death on the wind.

"Easy!" Longarm said in a soothing voice.

But the roan was spooked. It tried to wheel away from the smell of death and run, but Longarm got the animal under control and rode it back down the slope until he came to a stand of pinyon. He tied the agitated mustang, then slipped his Winchester from his saddle boot. Perhaps the movement he'd just seen out of the corner of his eye had been a wounded mustang trying to return to water, but maybe it was also one of the horse killers.

Longarm hurried back up the steep slope, and when he reached the ridge, he dropped and carefully scanned every square inch of the entire valley and the heavy encircling sagebrush. Whatever movement had caught his eye had disappeared, but although the earth was very warm, Longarm did not move a muscle. Flies buzzed, the buzzards continued to circle overhead, and Longarm displayed the kind of patience that was necessary for a man-hunter to stay alive.

It was nearly an hour before Longarm again caught the hint of movement. It was little more than a flicker of brown against the color of beige, but it was enough to tell Longarm that there was a man rather than another mustang in the tall brush that ringed the valley floor.

The minutes dragged on, and Longarm could hear his roan nervously pawing the earth. It was clear that Longarm would have to start the action, and so he eased back from the crest of the hill. When he was no longer skylighted, Longarm moved about three hundred yards and then returned to the ridge, hoping that he might be able to see his quarry better.

The mustang killer didn't seem to be aware that he was being watched. He emerged from the brush carrying two dead jackrabbits, probably caught in snares. Longarm watched the man plod over to his campfire, and then sit down heavily on the grass and remove a large Bowie knife from the sheath he carried on his belt. Quick as anything, the man was cutting and tearing the pelt off one of the jackrabbits. He gutted the animal and dropped it on the grass, looking up at the circling buzzards and raising his knife in a gesture of defiance.

Minutes later, the second jackrabbit was also skinned and the man, a filthy heavyset fellow with a black beard, vanished back into the brush, probably to gather firewood. Longarm figured it was now or never. It would take a considerable amount of time for him to ride around behind the mustang killer, and even then he would not have been that much closer. And while Longarm was within rifle range, the distance was too far to guarantee that he'd be able to just wound the man rather than kill him.

So Longarm jumped up and started trotting down toward the valley floor, keeping his eyes on where the man had disappeared and hoping that he would be gone until Longarm was in position to catch him by surprise.

That didn't happen. The mustang killer emerged from the heavy brush carrying an armload of firewood. When he saw Longarm, he dropped everything and his hand streaked for the gun on his hip.

"Freeze," Longarm shouted, throwing the Winchester to his shoulder and taking aim. "Don't do it!"

But the man was a fool and didn't heed Longarm's advice. He was determined to go for his six-gun and take a bullet for his trouble. Longarm tried for a shoulder shot, and when his rifle boomed, he saw his target spin completely around and fall, clutching his right shoulder.

"You sonofabitch!" the man squealed as he writhed around on the grass in pain. "You shot me!"

Longarm went over and disarmed the man, then stepped back and surveyed him for a minute before drawling,

"Well, I see that at least your damned hearing is good. Why didn't you do like I ordered?"

"Because I hate taking orders!"

"Nobody likes 'em," Longarm agreed, "but everyone has to answer to someone. Now, if you'll lift your hand off from that hole I put in your shoulder, I'll take a look at the damage."

"The hell you will!"

"Suit yourself," Longarm said, reluctantly concluding that this man was not one of the Elko bank robbers.

Longarm momentarily dismissed the man and began to sniff around, studying tracks and reading signs. He was especially careful to study the camp and when he was finished, he walked over to the wounded man and said, "Mister, I'm no Apache, but it appears to me like there were at least four or five others here besides you up until a day or two ago."

"What business is that of yours?" the man choked. "What do you want?"

"Oh," Longarm said, producing his badge, "I forgot to show you this. I'm a deputy marshal and I'm on the trail of three murdering jackals that robbed the Elko bank."

"Well, I ain't one of 'em! So you shot me for no damned good reason!"

Longarm shook his head. "That isn't exactly true. I shot you because I think you *are* connected with the men I'm hunting. And even if you aren't, I'd wager anything that you know who I'm talking about."

"What I *do* know is that I'm bleeding like a stuck pig!"

"It'll stop if you let me put a bandage on it. Either that, or you can plug the hole with one of your fingers."

The mustang killer glared at him. "Marshal, Hell will freeze over before I tell you a damned thing!"

"That's fine with me. You got a horse?"

"No."

"How come?"

"He ran off last night," the man admitted, looking disgusted. "These rotting mustangs made him sort of crazy and he got loose and just ran the hell off."

Longarm clucked his tongue. "That's a real pity. A man with a bullet in his shoulder probably isn't going to feel like walking thirty or forty miles back to Whiskey Creek for help."

"Walk?" The man shook his head. "Mister, I couldn't walk out of this little valley!"

"Where are they?"

"Who?"

"The bank robbers. Where are they mustanging?"

The wounded man grimaced. "I told you that I don't know what you're talking about!"

"Suit yourself," Longarm said, turning to head back to get his horse.

"You gonna leave me?"

"I am." Longarm broke stride. "Ordinarily, I'd arrest you for resisting arrest. But then, I suppose I really should have told you that I was a federal law officer before I put a slug in your shoulder."

"You damn right you should have!"

"But on the other hand," Longarm said, "I don't have much use for anyone who'd shoot mustangs, especially colts and fillies, just for their hides and tails. It's a real sorry business and one you need to think about quitting."

"You sonofabitch!" the man screamed, coming after Longarm. "I'll die out here without a doctor!"

"No, you won't," Longarm said, motioning toward the ripe and rotting carcasses. "You've got enough horse meat to keep yourself in business for at least a week before it all completely rots in this heat. But you might have to fight off the wolves, coyotes, and a bobcat or two."

"Wait!"

Longarm was almost ready to step into the brush and

climb up over the low ridge that cratered the valley. "Yeah?"

"The three men you're after? They're up in the Ruby Mountains about twenty miles east of here."

"That's better. What is your name?"

"Ralph."

"What are the names of the others?"

The man's face revealed the inner struggle that he waged trying to chose between loyalty and his own welfare. Welfare won. "Ed Williams, Tag Becker, and Phil Pate."

"You're sure?"

"Of course I'm sure! They were just here the day before yesterday. We're all working together, but them three are the only ones that rob banks."

"I'm going to give you the benefit of that doubt," Longarm told Ralph. "And that's why I'm leaving you to get yourself out of this fix on your own."

"I'll die!"

"There's nothing wrong with your legs, mister. So just quit whining and start walking."

"What about that bandage?"

"It'll have to come out of your shirt, not mine," Longarm told Ralph as he decided that his conscience wouldn't allow him to just walk away.

Longarm tore a strip out of the mustang killer's shirt, and then he went to the spring and doused the rag in cold water.

"Now you just hold still while I have a good look at this shoulder."

A moment later, Longarm's eyebrows raised as he inspected the bullet wound. Then he said, "My, my."

"What!" Ralph exclaimed with alarm. "Did your slug hit anything that'll kill me?"

"Nope, but it went all the way through and that's good news for you."

"It is?"

"Sure. The bleeding has probably already cleaned the hole out, and after we get the bleeding stopped, you'll have a better than even chance of making it."

"Thank gawd," Ralph breathed. "But I sure don't have the strength to walk for help."

"Sometimes a man has to try and do what he doesn't think is possible. Sometimes, if he does that, he'll even surprise himself."

"Not me. I'm hurt too bad. I got to stay here near the water and this meat."

"Then go ahead and stay put," Longarm told the man. "If you've told me the truth, I'll capture or kill those bank robbers and pass back through here and pick you up."

"They'll do the killing, not you," Ralph said without a moment's hesitation. "They're marksmen and they're tougher than boot leather. Not only the three you want, but the ones that they're riding with."

"And how many, exactly, would that be?"

There was a long hesitation, and Longarm had to repeat, "How many?"

"There's two more. Sonny Lonigan and Art Spense. They're real tough boys."

"Then it's five," Longarm said, wanting to make very sure that there was no misunderstanding.

"Yeah. We were six, but I stayed here."

"Why?"

"I was supposed to be scouting for more mustangs. But my horse ran off and I've just been cooling my heels until you came along and messed everything up."

"Sometimes," Longarm said, unable to generate much sympathy, "a man's situation just goes from bad to worse in a hell of a hurry and there ain't a damn thing that he can do about it."

"I don't want to listen to your cheap philosophy," Ralph said, gritting his teeth. "I want a doctor!"

"Then you'd best get to hoofin' it," Longarm said. "I'll

stop by on the way back through, but I still think you ought to try and make the walk. That bullet hole ought to be clean considering how much blood you've lost, but a man never knows when he'll contract lead poisoning."

Longarm turned his back on the man and started up the slope. He was almost to the crest when he thought he heard something metallic click behind him. He turned just a moment before Ralph unleashed a .50-caliber ball from his big, single-shot buffalo rifle. The ball missed Longarm by inches, and he swore he could feel its hot breath pass his cheek.

"Just for that," Longarm shouted, "I'm going to arrest you if you're still here when I come back! It's against the law to shoot at a federal marshal!"

"Fuck you and your laws!" Ralph screamed in a fit of rage.

Longarm could have gone back down and shot Ralph again, but his heart just wasn't in it. The truth of the matter was that he had three real killers to track down and bring to justice. Oh, yeah, along with their two friends, who would most surely decide to throw in to the fight.

Longarm topped the rise before Ralph could get another ball into his rifle and have a second chance of ventilating his hide. He trotted down the hill, untied his own fine mustang, and swung into the saddle.

This had not been a bad stop. He'd lost a little time, true enough. But in the process, he'd also gained the names of the three bank robbers and murderers that he was bound and determined to bring to justice.

Ed Williams. Tag Becker. Phil Pate. They were names that Longarm wasn't about to forget. Nor would he forget the names of the other two mustang killers that he'd have to deal with. Sonny Lonigan and Art Spense.

Five against one, but he had the element of surprise.

Longarm was about four hundred yards off and riding fast when he heard the distant retort of the buffalo rifle once more. He twisted around in his saddle and thought that Ralph was wasting lead, until the mustang suddenly shied as a lead ball struck a rock and ricocheted betwecn its legs.

''Damn nice shooting for a man with a bad shoulder,'' Longarm muttered. It was a warning, he thought, of the kind of marksmen that he would be facing somewhere ahead in the wild Ruby Mountains of Nevada.

Chapter 13

Longarm was pushing the big roan mustang hard, and he knew it. Still, he didn't feel there was much of a choice. Mustang hunters would never light in one place for very long because, as soon as they'd killed off one band, they'd have to scout up another. Mustangs were territorial creatures, and their separate ranges could encompass hundreds of square miles. They were always moving, bound only by the location of water in this arid, high desert country nestled along the western slopes of the Ruby Mountains.

On the third morning out of Whiskey Creek, Longarm heard a crashing sound in the brush and wheeled his horse for cover. He quickly dismounted and ducked behind a rock, thinking maybe he'd accidentally blundered upon the mustang killers. Instead of the outlaws he expected, a colt emerged from the undergrowth. It was only a few weeks old, big-eyed, spindly-legged, and starving. When it saw Longarm and his roan gelding, it snorted and retreated a few yards, but it was lame and very weak.

"Hey," Longarm called, rummaging around in his saddlebags for something to feed the little fella.

There wasn't anything but a few dried apples, so he grabbed two and dismounted. He tied his horse to a piece of brush, then squatted on his heels and studied the emaciated colt. "Don't be afraid of me. What happened to your rump?"

But even as he asked and the colt moved closer, Longarm realized the answer to his own question. The colt had been shot at and a heavy-caliber ball had furrowed deep across its rump, slicing through sinew of both buttocks. Longarm could see that the bullet wound was not fatal, but that it had become infected and was causing the colt a lot of pain. In time, if it wasn't treated, blowflies would leave larvae in the wound and it would become filled with maggots. After a month or two, the colt would sicken and die.

"Come on over here," Longarm said in his most soothing voice. "I won't hurt you, but I damn sure want to stop the fellas who did this miserable job on your hind end."

The colt was wobbly and dull-eyed with pain and fever. The closer that Longarm looked, the more he thought that he might already be too late to save the colt.

"I just want to see if I can help you," Longarm said, inching forward with the dried apples extended in his hand. "Come on now."

The colt definitely smelled the dried apples, and it must have at least had some appetite because it inched forward. Behind Longarm, the roan mustang gelding nickered, as if voicing equine encouragement. When the colt's upper lip curled and it tried to bite at the apple, Longarm lunged forward, tackling the skittish colt. It struggled, but was so weak that it gave him no real battle.

"Sorry for the rough stuff," Longarm said, "but I couldn't afford to have you run away. I'm not carrying a lariat and I'd never catch you in all that brush."

Longarm tied the colt's forelegs and hind legs, then sat down and closely examined its bullet wound. It looked and smelled awful, but Longarm thought that the wound could be cleaned out, and maybe even sewn shut if he had had a needle and thread.

"Don't you worry," he promised. "I'm going to do my best to put a little meat on your bones."

Longarm had ridden past a stream less than a mile back, so he picked up the colt and hoisted it across his saddle. The poor thing didn't weigh much, and there was no struggle at all in its starving body.

Fifteen minutes later, Longarm had the colt stretched out beside the stream and was cleaning the wound. It was pretty nasty, but he'd dealt with worse. No maggots, just lots of corrupted flesh that had to be cut and scraped away so that new, healthy tissue could fill in and the colt's wound would heal properly.

The wounded and suffering mustang cost Longarm three hours, but that was only the beginning. Unable to leave the animal unattended, he draped it across his saddle and remounted. It was a real tight fit, and if the colt hadn't been so weak and compliant, it would never have worked. As it was, the colt just laid its head down and accepted whatever fate awaited.

That evening, Longarm ran into a pair of prospectors, or rather, they stepped out of their mine in the side of a hill and surprised him. The prospectors were also startled and jumped for their rifles, which were leaning up against some shoring timbers beside the entrance.

"Hold up there!" Longarm shouted. "I'm a United States deputy marshal and I need your help!"

The two men snatched up their rifles, and Longarm also filled his hand, but he knew he was at a serious disadvantage trying to hang onto the colt, and that made him angry. "Don't shoot! I said that I was a federal lawman!"

"All right, show us your damned badge!"

Longarm holstered his gun and tried to shift the colt forward so that he could reach into his pants pocket and drag out his badge. The mustang struggled and Longarm lost his grip. The next thing he knew, he held the colt by only one thin hind leg while it dangled from his saddle, thrashing and making awful sounds.

"Dammit!" Longarm shouted at the pair. "Come on over and give me a hand!"

The prospectors were old and suspicious, but when they saw the thin little mustang hanging upside down and frightened witless, they hurried over and grabbed him, then gently eased him to the ground.

"What the hell happened to him?" one of the prospectors demanded when he saw the nasty bullet wound across the colt's hindquarters.

"Mustang killers," Longarm explained as he dismounted. "I found this little fella and doctored him up as best I could."

"You need to close the hole up," one of the prospectors said. "That's too big a hole to leave open."

"I know," Longarm said, "but I didn't have any needle or thread."

"We've got some," the other prospector growled. "Hank, you know where we put that needle and thread?"

"I sure do," Hank replied. "It's in that little wood box. We also got some liniment and bandages. Might be that a little whiskey will clean things up proper."

Longarm nodded and introduced himself. This prospector's name was Ernie and he seemed to be the one in charge. Ernie was big and sported a full beard and silver hair down to his shoulders. He had bushy eyebrows and the palest blue eyes that Longarm had ever seen.

"You hungry?" Ernie asked as they held the struggling colt to the earth.

"I might be when this is done," Longarm answered, suddenly realizing that he had not had any food since morning.

Hank was quick and sure with the needle and thread, and the mustang didn't seem to even feel the suturing. Hank looked up after he was satisfied and said, "I don't think I need to do this little fella's other cheek. The other side's bullet wound isn't near so deep.''

''Then douse it with a little whiskey—but not too much,'' Ernie added quickly. ''And let's see if we can rustle up some food for this starvin' little critter.''

''I gave him some dried apples,'' Longarm told them. ''In fact, he would have ate every last one I had, but I was afraid of him getting the trots and making a hell of a mess down the side of me and my horse.''

''I can understand that,'' Hank said in a solemn voice. ''Ernie and I have a couple of burros and we've brought some oats and cracked corn. I expect this little horse will eat both.''

Longarm felt a wash of relief. He hadn't had the colt with him even a single day, but he'd already become attached to it. For the last several hours, he had been torn between his duty as a lawmen to bring in the Elko bank robbers and killers, and his feelings as a human being toward the suffering of a helpless newborn animal. The colt might be just a worthless mustang scrub, but it was suffering and Longarm wanted it to have a chance to live.

''I'm after three men who robbed the bank in Elko,'' Longarm explained, finally getting around to showing the pair his marshal's badge. ''And I heard that they had joined up with a bunch of hard-riding and straight-shooting men who are killing mustangs in these parts.''

''And you expect that they shot this little fella?'' Ernie asked, opening a gunnysack of oats and offering a small handful to the colt, who greedily devoured them.

''I'm not sure if they were the same group or not,'' Longarm admitted. ''The only thing I do know is that I'd like to put a stop to this kind of thing in addition to capturing those three bank robbers. Can you help me?''

''How do you mean?'' Hank asked. ''We're not manhunters.''

"I know that," Longarm said, "but I was hoping that maybe you've seen this bunch."

He described the three men that he was after, and ended by saying, "The names of the bank robbers and killers are Ed Williams, Tag Becker, and Phil Pate. Though I don't know which is which."

"Never heard of 'em," Ernie said, looking to his partner, who shook his head.

"And," Longarm continued, "they've thrown in with a couple of men whose names are Sonny Lonigan and Art Spense."

At the mention of those last two names, both prospectors sat up a little straighter and nodded rapidly. "Now we do know that pair," Ernie admitted. "And they are mean sonofabitches."

"Have you seen them in the last few days?"

"Saw 'em about a week ago," Hank said. "They said they were going to hunt wild mustangs over by Soda Springs."

"How far is that?"

"About forty miles east. But mustanging isn't like mining, you know. A mine, she stays in the same place, but mustangs like to ramble."

"I know that," Longarm said. "Were those two men working by themselves, or in the company of others?"

"Come to think of it," Ernie replied, "there were three other men with 'em. They stayed on their horses, but they did ask how we was doin' with our mine."

"Course we told 'em that the mine wasn't payin' off and we was about to quit working here and move on again," Hank added.

"Of course," Longarm said. "To say otherwise would have been extremely foolish, as you're well aware. Were they heavily armed and well mounted?"

"Damn right they were," Ernie said. "They all had them big hunting rifles. They didn't say they used 'em to kill mustangs, but we knew that's why they were carryin' 'em.''

Longarm passed another hour with the prospectors. Like most of their kind, they were a little odd, sometimes talking to themselves or just staring off into the distance. But they were also good and honest men.

''Well,'' Longarm said, finishing off a cup of coffee and some salt pork and leftover biscuits from that morning, ''I need to be traveling.''

''What you going to do with that little colt?'' Ernie asked, trying to sound disinterested.

Longarm put his hands on his hips. ''I don't know.''

''Maybe we could have him? But he'll probably die.''

''I know,'' Longarm said, ''and it wouldn't be fair that you should put a lot of oats and corn in him for nothing.''

''Aw,'' Hank said, stroking the colt's neck. ''We can always buy more. The important thing is that this little jasper needs a couple of friends. Our burros will cozy up to him. In fact, my guess is that this colt will soon be thinking that he *is* a burro.''

''So you really want to go to all that bother, even though he'll probably just up and die?''

''Why not?'' Ernie said. ''We can't just leave him for the bone-pickin' coyotes!''

''All right then,'' Longarm said, as if it were really a tough decision. ''You go ahead and keep him. But I'll expect you to nursemaid him back to good health.''

''We'll do our level best.''

''And once he's healthy again, you can't just turn him loose if he gets to be a bother.''

''No, sir!'' they answered in the same breath.

''Fair enough then,'' Longarm said. ''What are you going to name him?''

They both shrugged and Longarm said, ''You'll think of something. He may just turn out to be a pretty fine horse someday.''

"He could be handsome," Ernie said. "At least, he would be if his ass wasn't half shot off and he wasn't so damned skinny."

"That's right," Hank agreed. "He'd look just fine except for all them burrs in his mane and tail. All he needs is an awful lot of brushing."

Longarm nodded his head in agreement. "He does for a fact. And when I come riding back through these parts, I'll expect to either see a little grave or a brushed and shiny little colt that thinks he's a burro."

"Fair enough!" Ernie said with a wide grin splitting his silver beard. "But if you're going to ride after five men, then I don't expect we'll ever see you again anyway. They'll kill you for certain, Marshal."

"That's it!" Hank cried, slapping his knee. "We'll call the little starvin' bugger Marshal. What do you think?"

Longarm chuckled. "Marshal is a fine name for him. I've never had a horse named after me. In fact, I've never had anything named after me."

"Well," Ernie said, "neither have I."

Longarm was eager to leave. He'd spent the better part of a day helping to save the colt, but now it was time to get down to the business of man-hunting. "Are there any landmarks that will tell me I'm about to reach Soda Springs before I get there?" he asked.

"Yeah," Hank said, after a moment. "There's a big white slash in the side of the mountains. Must be alkali or something. But you'll see it a good ten miles before you get to Soda Springs. The springs itself is down in a little depression, and you won't find it until you come over a rise of land and then drop right down on the top of 'er."

"Thanks," Longarm said, remounting his fine mustang gelding. "One more thing," he said before riding off.

"What's that?"

"If you see those men again, don't mention that I'm

looking for them and don't mention that I brought that colt to you.''

''What would we tell 'em if they asked?'' Hank wanted to know.

''Just say that the colt wandered in and you decided to take care of it. They might want to kill it for its tail, but I expect you'll have something to say about that.''

''We'd put up a hell of a fight before we'd let 'em cut the little bugger's tail off,'' Hank said, looking at his partner, who grimly nodded.

Satisfied that the colt was in good and protective hands, Longarm rode off at a gallop. He would not reach Soda Springs until tomorrow, but that was just fine. As long as he finally found his Elko outlaws and put a stop to this damned mustang hunting, he would be more than satisfied.

But that, he knew was going to be a tall, tall order.

Chapter 14

Longarm rode late that night, and got an early start the next morning. As he moved eastward, the country became greener as the elevation increased. Instead of just pinyon and juniper pines, there were fir and even aspen crowding the canyon streams. This was beautiful country, and Longarm's mustang seemed energized by the crisper air despite the long miles they had already traveled.

About noon, Longarm found what he had been looking for, the gash of white that marked a mountainside. "Not much farther now," he told his mustang.

He was about to say more when he heard the distant rumble of heavy rifles. Had Longarm not known about the big hunting weapons his quarry carried, he might even have thought that he was hearing thunder, except that this rifle fire was sporadic and disjointed.

A hardness settled in the pit of Longarm's stomach and he touched his heels to the roan, willing it to race forward. His mount was surefooted and well conditioned. It galloped for about three miles until the firing died, and Longarm knew that he was very close to the mustang killers. He trotted to a low rise of land, and dismounted to tie the roan and move cautiously forward.

What he saw when he topped the rise was five men totally occupied in their grisly work of skinning a dozen mustangs, three of which were yearlings. The mustang killers had already hacked off the tails of their victims. The hardness in Longarm's stomach turned to burning fury, and he retreated to his horse in order to collect both the Big Fifty that Duncan had given him and his Winchester. Those two rifles, coupled with his six-gun, would give him a lot of firepower, and he might need all of it that he could muster. As he hurried back to the ridge, Longarm was not in the least bit sure how he was going to get the drop on five men, but guessed that he would figure out something before he hiked over the hill and forced a showdown.

Just before he reached the crest of the hill, Longarm made sure that his .50-caliber Sharps breechloader was ready to fire. He also levered a shell into the Winchester, and then he checked his pistol. It was his intention to try to keep the mustang killers from reaching their big-bored hunting rifles. They were packing pistols, but as long as he could keep them from their deadly accurate high-powered buffalo rifles, he thought he would retain an important advantage.

"All right," he said to himself when he was sure that everything was ready and in order, "here goes."

Longarm stepped over the crest of the ridge and sat down, laying the Winchester at his side and butting the Sharps to his shoulder. The men below were so intent on their bloody skinning work that they were not aware of his presence. Longarm studied the five men closely, and was able to identify the Elko bank robbers and assassins. If this turned into a fight, Longarm wanted to make sure that he dropped those three men first.

Well, he thought, there was no sense in putting this business off any longer. Longarm bellowed, "All of you are under arrest! Hands up! I'm United States Deputy Marshal Custis—"

They were all within a hundred yards of Longarm, working wherever they'd dropped a running mustang. When Longarm's voice cut through the valley's silence, the men below jerked their heads up and stared for a moment in shocked silence. One of the robbers was the first to react. He shouted something and went for his six-gun, even though it was ineffective at this range. Longarm had been expecting a fight, and he knew he had to whittle the odds down in a hurry if he had any chance of survival. His Sharps rifle slid sideways about an inch and Longarm fired quickly. His bullet struck the man in the chest and knocked him back into the dead mustang he'd been skinning.

The other hunters bolted like quail for their own rifles, and Longarm knew he could not afford to let them become equally well armed. He snatched up his Winchester and tracked a second robber, then squeezed his trigger. The man was reaching for his rifle, but never quite touched it as Longarm's bullet entered just under his armpit. He went down kicking, and Longarm levered another shot into the Winchester and searched for the last Elko bank robber. But this man was sprinting up the valley toward his horse. Longarm fired at him but missed, and by that time the other two mustang killers, Lonigan and Spense, had their own big rifles and were leaping behind the bodies of a couple of dead mustangs.

Longarm knew that he was a sitting duck and that he was up against superior marksmen. There was nothing to do but to get back over the ridge before one of the men below put a bullet through his hide. He jumped up with both his rifles and sprinted headlong for the ridge, some thirty feet behind him. A deep-throated boom was followed an instant later by a searing fire along the top of Longarm's shoulder. A second boom sent Longarm diving over the crest of the ridge, and he knew that he had almost lost his life. Rolling a few feet, Longarm came to rest and then quickly reloaded his Sharps.

He was not pleased, because he'd squandered his element

of surprise and only killed two of the five men. Not that he had any real bone to pick with Lonigan and Spense, but he had expected that he'd have to get through the pair of them in order to deal with the men he really wanted.

Longarm finished reloading the Sharps and scrambled back to the crest the hill. He removed his Stetson and peered over the top to see that Lonigan and Spense were hunkered down behind their dead mustangs and that the man he really wanted, the third robber, was galloping off toward the Ruby Mountains as if Satan were hot on his heels.

Longarm ground his teeth in fury. "You men down below!" he shouted. "Lonigan and Spense!"

"What do you want?" one of them cried.

"I told you I was the law, dammit! I was after Becker, Williams, and Pate for bank robbery and murder."

"We didn't rob no bank or murder anyone!"

"Then throw down your arms."

The two men held a quick conference. Longarm couldn't make out their exact words, but he could hear them trying to come to some agreement.

"Show us your badge, Marshal!"

Longarm showed them his damned badge.

"What are you going to do with us if we surrender?"

"I'm going to put you out of business," Longarm shouted. "And if you won't settle for that, I'll either put you in a grave or in prison. Your choice!"

The pair started to argue. Longarm didn't know which was Lonigan and which was Spense, but it was clear they were having a serious difference of opinion. Finally, the darker-complected of the pair raised his head from behind his dead mustang and shouted, "What's wrong with this business?"

"Mustangs belong to the federal government and I'm a federal officer."

"But what—"

"And I'm putting you the hell out of this damned business. Now throw out your rifles or prepare to face the consequences."

It took them almost a full minute to finally decide to throw their rifles out, and Longarm was more than a little relieved when he stood up with his Sharps and went down to collect their weapons.

"Stand up and put your hands over your head!" Longarm ordered when he drew nearer. "Now!"

Lonigan and Spense exchanged hurried glances, and that was when Longarm knew that the pair had no intention of surrendering anything. They both jumped up with their pistols blazing, but they were not nearly so good with six-guns as they were with their rifles. If they had been, Longarm would probably have been hit. As it was, he drilled one of them with the Sharps, and then his hand flashed to his six-gun as he dove for the ground, rolling and firing each time he was on his belly.

He unleashed three bullets, but only two of them were accurate. One hit the mustang killer in the shoulder and the other in the gut, causing the man to collapse to his knees and howl. Longarm hurried over and took the gun from the man, saying, "I need to look at that wound."

"Go to hell!" he screamed.

Longarm went over to check the rest of the men, and they were all dead. He turned his eyes up the valley, but the third robber was long gone. Longarm returned to the dying man. "What is your name?"

"Sonny . . . Lonigan."

"You are a fool, Sonny. I wasn't after you and Spense. I just wanted those other three."

"You're the law," Sonny grunted. "I hate every last one of you bastards and I will till my dying day."

"Which is this one," Longarm said. "There's no way that you are going to survive that wound, Sonny."

"You got any whiskey?" the man choked.

"Nope. Have you?"

"Some over yonder by the camp," Sonny breathed. "I need a drink."

Longarm surveyed the man. Lonigan was now on his side, knees pulled up close to his chest. His face was gray with pain, and Longarm knew that the man could not possibly last more than an hour or two. He wanted to leave and go after the third robber, but common decency demanded that he remain with Sonny until the man died.

"I need a drink, dammit!" Sonny wheezed.

"All right," Longarm said, going over to the camp and rummaging around. It only took him a few minutes to find the whiskey and a saddlebag full of greenbacks. When Longarm returned to Sonny, he said, "How come you boys didn't just spend all this money?"

Sonny took a long pull on the bottle and glared at him. "We didn't even know they *had* money until a couple of days ago. Soon as we found that out, we was all for heading back to Whiskey Creek, but them three from Elko wouldn't hear of that. They was greedy and worried that someone like you would be coming along their back trail."

"You should have cut away from them."

"We was going to, soon as we could figure out how to get away with their money," the dying man confessed.

He rolled his head back and forth, gazing at dead horses and dead men. "They all finished?"

"One got away," Longarm said, "but I'll track him down and bring him to justice."

"That's Phil Pate! I hope he puts a bullet in *your* gut!" Sonny gasped before he took another long, shuddering drink. "You sonofabitch, this wasn't our fight!"

"You made it your fight when you decided to go for your guns."

Sonny closed his eyes. He was panting and in such pain that he had to grit his teeth between short bursts of words. "My only satisfaction is that you took a bullet."

"Just a flesh wound," Longarm said, glancing down at the top of his right shoulder and then sitting cross-legged on the ground. "It won't slow me down."

Sonny didn't answer, but instead worked at the bottle until it was empty. Longarm watched the man grow steadily weaker, and once he asked, "You got anyone you want me to let know you died?"

"Only ones that will mourn my passin' are whores. Got no family that I care to speak about."

"Too bad," Longarm said.

"Will you bury us?"

"Don't have a shovel," Longarm said. "Nothing to dig with."

"Then at least tie us across our saddles and haul us back to town for buryin'!"

"No time for that," Longarm said. "Maybe on my way back. But my first job is to stop Phil Pate."

The dying man sobbed. "By the time you kill him and come back, the wolves and the buzzards will have eaten us!"

"I'm sorry," Longarm said. "If I come across a prospector or someone out here with a shovel, I'll send him here to bury you. But that's the best that I can do."

"Bastard!"

Longarm looked away for a minute, then made a decision. He came to his feet and picked up his rifles. "I'm leaving now," he said. "I don't think my company means anything to you, and Pate is getting farther away."

"Give me a gun!"

Longarm shook his head. "You'd just try to shoot me. You're that damned bad. You'd try and shoot me in the gut."

"You're right, lawman! I'd want you to burn in Hell just before me."

"Too bad," Longarm said.

"Shoot me!" Sonny begged. "Don't leave me like this!"

"I'll leave you a pistol with one bullet in it," Longarm said, walking about ten feet and then ejecting all the bullets of a revolver into his pocket except one. "It might take a couple of minutes to reach it, but you can."

"You're no better than we was! You're wolf-mean and heartless. The only difference between you and me is that you're wearing a badge."

"No, it isn't," Longarm corrected. "Another big difference between you and me is that I wouldn't shoot mustangs for their hides and tails."

"What in the hell do you think happened to the gawddamn buffalo?" Sonny cried.

The question caught Longarm by surprise, and he knew that Sonny had a point. Scratching his jaw, Longarm said, "The buffalo hunters wiped out the great herds for their hides and that was also wrong. But it goes beyond that because a horse is more than a buffalo."

Sonny didn't understand, and when he tried to argue, he began to cough and could not speak. Longarm took a deep breath and moved the gun a little closer to the dying man.

"Maybe we are more alike than I care to admit," he said. "And maybe you never killed an innocent man before, though I expect you've killed plenty. The point is that you could have surrendered and you didn't. I could be the one dying and you the one walking away. It just turned out that I won and you lost."

Longarm left. He didn't feel good about the way this had turned out, but at least he was alive and sometimes, that was the best that a man could expect.

He was almost at the top of the ridge when he heard the Colt .45 crash and saw a spray of dirt and grass erupt just beyond him.

Longarm twisted around to see Sonny raise a clenched fist at him. Longarm shook his head and waved good-bye, then hurried down for his horse. Phil Pate was a good hour ahead of him and time was wasting.

Chapter 15

Longarm was more than a little dismayed when he found Phil Pate's tracks and discovered that the man had taken an extra horse. Pate would be able to use two horses, switching back and forth to make his escape faster. There being no help for that, Longarm set off on the trail of the last bank robber confident that his roan mustang could and would overtake Pate within the next twenty-four hours.

Longarm had no idea where his man was heading, except that it was into the Ruby Mountains. Perhaps Pate was thinking that he could escape if he got higher up in the rocks, and there was also the possibility that Pate was thinking ambush. It would be easier to ambush a pursuer up in the heavy timber than it would have been down on the sage-and-pinyon-covered hills.

Longarm rode until dark, when he could no longer follow the tracks, which he judged to be no more than a few hours old. He built a large campfire, and then he fluffed up his bedroll to make it look like he was sleeping inside. Longarm moved into the shadows and hunkered down to see if his bait would be taken by the man he hunted. It was Longarm's experience that a fugitive on the run, if he thought he could double back and kill his pursuer, often made the attempt.

The mountain air was chill, and Longarm regretted that he had left the summer heat of Whiskey Creek without bringing a heavy jacket. He was cold and uncomfortable, and tried to at least keep his hands warm so he could use a gun if the need suddenly arose.

Longarm must have dozed off because, sometime well after midnight, he awoke with a start to the sound of gunfire. Not fully awake, Longarm snatched up his six-gun and rolled forward onto his belly. He knuckled the sleep from his eyes and stared toward his camp, not twenty feet away. It was difficult to see anything. The overhanging branches of tall pines blocked the moon, and the only lights in the sky at all were a few pinprick stars. Even the campfire, which Longarm had taken pains to make extra bright, now burned low and smoky.

Longarm held his breath and waited. Pate would want to enter the camp and make sure that his pursuer was finished. Furthermore, he'd also want to loot the camp of weapons and food as well as his victim's horse and saddle. No, Longarm thought, Pate isn't going to run away now. Not as long as he thinks I'm bleeding to death in that bedroll.

And sure enough, Longarm saw the bank robber's crouched silhouette emerge out of the darkness. For some reason, Pate was tiptoeing forward, as if he expected that the sound of his footfall would awaken his dead or dying victim. When he came to within ten feet of the bedroll, Pate chuckled and emptied his gun.

"You stupid—"

"Hold up there!" Longarm said, jumping to his feet and cocking back the hammer of his Colt. "I just *hate* to be wrongly insulted."

Pate twisted halfways around, his finger squeezing his trigger, but the hammer clicked on an empty cylinder. "Why, you sly sonofabitch," he breathed.

Longarm moved forward. "I don't know how long you've been robbing banks and shooting down innocent folks, but I've been hunting you low and miserable types long enough to learn a few tricks."

"I never shot any of those folks in Elko," Pate said quickly. "I was stuffing money in a pair of saddlebags when Tag and Ed opened fire."

"You can tell that to a judge and a jury."

"Hell, I don't even have the damned money we took!"

"I know," Longarm said. "You were so scared that you ran out on your friends. I've got it now and it'll be returned to Elko. Maybe that will make the difference between hanging and a life sentence in the Nevada State Prison at Carson City, but I wouldn't bet on it."

"You killed all the others by yourself?"

"Like I said," Longarm repeated, "I've learned a few tricks, and I had the advantage of surprise."

"Lonigan and Spense weren't even in on that bank job! You killed a couple of innocent men."

"They tried to kill *me*," Longarm said. "I gave all of you the chance to surrender and you decided to do it the hard way. Now put your hands up and turn around slow."

Pate did as he was told, and Longarm quickly had the killer's hands bound behind his back. Satisfied that Pate wasn't going to give him any trouble, he said, "Lay down on your belly."

"Huh?"

Longarm kicked the man's legs out from under him. "I said lay down," he ordered. "Mister, I'm going to warn you right now that I don't have much tolerance for your type. You killed innocent people in Elko and you came over here and slaughtered good mustang ponies."

"A man has to make a living."

"Aw, shut up," Longarm growled, tying the man's feet and then drawing both hands and feet together so that Pate could barely move.

"Hey, this hurts!"

"Life hurts," Longarm said. "Now, I'm going to crawl

back into my blankets and get a few hours of sleep before morning. Then we're riding back to Elko, where I'll hand you over to the local authorities."

"I'd rather stand trial in Whiskey Creek," Pate whined. "I won't get any justice in Elko!"

"You'll get justice."

"I can't stay in this position while you sleep! My hands are going numb and my gut is stretched. It's tearing me up inside like barbed wire."

"If you make a sound and wake me up, I'll put you out of your damned misery," Longarm warned. "Be easier all the way around to shoot you and be done with it. Three bank robbers and killers, all dead men."

Pate gulped and averted his face while Longarm hauled his bullet-riddled bedroll back into the trees. "Pate, you owe me a new bedroll!"

"Damn you!" Pate sobbed. "I'm in pain!"

"If you think you're in pain now, just wait until tomorrow," Longarm said, closing his eyes and dropping off into a doze that would carry him into daybreak.

Pate was either dead or asleep the next morning when the first light of day filtered through the overhanging trees and stirred Longarm into wakefulness. He had slept with his gun next to his hand, but he needn't have worried. Pate was a weakling and a coward, and not all that resourceful or determined. Longarm knew that the man would whine and bitch all the way back to Elko, constantly proclaiming his innocence.

Not wanting to listen to him any longer than was necessary, Longarm went off and found the outlaw's two horses. The lazy bastard hadn't even bothered to loosen their cinches, much less unsaddle them. Longarm found both animals grazing in a little meadow, and he led them back to his camp, then saddled his own fine mustang gelding and packed his gear behind his cantle.

He made a fire and boiled some coffee, then fried some

rabbit meat that the prospectors had given him after he'd left them the colt. When he'd eaten and had his second cup of coffee, he woke Pate up and dragged him over to a horse. Untying the man's feet, he boosted him into the saddle and then tied his boots to the stirrups.

"If you even think about running out on me," Longarm said, "I'll just ride you down and shoot you in the back, then dump your carcass alongside your friends."

Pate looked wan and shaky. "I'm mighty hungry and you didn't even give me time to piss before you threw me on this horse."

"Piss on yourself," Longarm growled, mounting his roan and taking a lead line he'd attached to the outlaw's good saddle horses. "We've got a lot of miles to cover."

On the way back, they passed by the valley where a swarm of vultures and buzzards were feeding on dead men and dead mustangs. Longarm's expression was grim and he said, "Pate, I don't expect you'd like me to lead you up there to the crest of that hill so you can say a last farewell to your friends."

"Hell, no!"

"Well," Longarm said, "if we had a shovel, I'd make you bury both the men and the mustangs. That would take a couple of days. But we don't have a shovel, so we'll just have to push on."

"I wouldn't go over into that valley if the devil himself had me by the throat."

Longarm didn't say much to that. He pushed on, smelling the stench of death and decay and hearing the raucous fighting cries of the birds of prey as they feasted.

The next day they camped at Soda Springs, and Longarm had the pleasure of seeing a band of free-running mustangs. Turning to Pate, he said, "At least you didn't have time to kill them all."

"Are you kidding?" his prisoner said. "There are fifty or sixty bands in this part of Nevada. A man could hunt them for ten years and they'd multiply faster than he could shoot 'em."

"That doesn't matter to me," Longarm said. "And it doesn't change the fact that the whole damned idea leaves a real bad taste in my mouth."

They arrived at Hank and Ernie's mine the following afternoon, and the two prospectors had to be restrained when Longarm told them that Phil Pate was one of the mustang killers.

"Easy, boys," Longarm said. "He's going to face the mighty justice of the law in Elko."

"Why bother," Ernie hissed as he went over to grab an old rope. "We can have ourselves a little necktie party right here and now!"

"Marshal!" Pate pleaded. "You can't let them hang me!"

"He's right," Longarm said. "Boys, I'm sworn to uphold the law and bring this man to trial. So why don't you just show me that colt I left behind and let's not trouble ourselves with things that cannot be."

The mention of the mustang colt caused a dramatic change in the two prospectors. Their hateful glowering vanished as they led Longarm and his prisoner up a small creek to a little corral that was hidden by a spring. When the colt saw Longarm, the animal snorted and danced away, rolling his eyes.

"Hey!" Longarm called with a huge smile. "Is that any way to treat the man that saved your shot-up little hide?"

Hank elbowed Longarm. "See those burros? They've taken to that runty orphan like a couple of fussy old hens. They watch out for Marshal, you bet they do."

"Glad to hear that," Longarm said. "And it appears that his rump is healing up clean. I can't see so many bony angles now either. I'd say you and Ernie are doing a first-class job with this little guy."

"What's the big damned fuss?" Pate snapped. "It's just

a miserable scrub mustang. Ain't worth so much as a laying hen or a turkey.''

Hank lunged for the outlaw's throat, and would have strangled Pate if Longarm hadn't pulled him off.

''Marshal Long, I think you had best get that sonofabitch outta our sight before we kill him.''

Longarm had been expecting to spend the night there, but now he realized that was not such a good idea. ''Let's ride,'' he said to Pate.

''But it's only a few hours until dark!''

''We're going to ride anyway,'' Longarm said, shoving his prisoner toward their horses.

As they prepared to ride, Longarm said, ''Hank. Ernie. You want to earn forty easy dollars?''

''Why, sure!'' Hank said, his face splitting into a wide grin. ''How?''

''There's four dead men over near Soda Springs. They're the ones that I went after. I'd like you to take picks and shovels and bury them.''

''That wouldn't be easy money,'' Hank said.

''Not easy at all,'' Ernie agreed.

''Maybe not,'' Longarm admitted. ''But it's a lot of money and it's a job that needs to be done.''

The pair thought a moment. Then Hank said, ''All right, Marshal Long, we'll do it. But cash in advance.''

Longarm paid them out of the Elko bank money, and then he left in a hurry, dragging Phil Pate and the extra horses along behind. He was thinking about seeing Donita again in Whiskey Creek. If she still wanted to come with him to Denver, that was all right too.

Chapter 16

Marshal Billy Wade was feeling on top of the world, or rather, Whiskey Creek. Everything had gone exactly as he'd expected during the election, and he now presided over a good city council—good meaning men who would do his bidding and who had appointed him in an official capacity as their town marshal.

"So, Boss," Whiskey Creek's new deputy marshal drawled, "which businesses are we going to start shakin' down first?"

Billy turned away from the window and scowled at Oliver Moody. "When I hired you as my deputy, I thought that I'd made it very clear that we aren't going to shake down anyone. What we are doing, Oliver, is offering *extra protection.*"

Oliver was a horse-faced man in his mid-thirties who had the unfortunate habit of picking his nose and never changing his clothes. He was disgusting, but fast with a gun and very loyal—qualities that Billy needed most at this particular stage of his plans. In time, Billy would get rid of Oliver one way or another and improve the quality of his help, but for right now, Oliver was willing to work cheap and follow orders without question. He was a bit rough and brutal, but he was effective, and Billy knew that the man was invaluable.

''Extra protection, huh,'' Oliver said, grinning to reveal that his front upper teeth were missing and those along both sides were dark with decay. ''I keep forgetting those fancy words you use to mean takin' the businessmen's money. Sorry, Boss.''

Oliver didn't look sorry at all. He was grinning and picking at his nose, and Billy looked away in disgust. Outside on the boardwalk, he could see that everyone had checked in their side arms and that things were calm and well under control. It hadn't been easy to get the miners to give up their weapons when they visited for a night on the town, but after a few stern lessons, they had finally seen fit to obey the law. And now, during the daytime, Whiskey Creek was as peaceful as a church picnic.

Unfortunately, there were still problems at night because the miners would get drunk and they'd haul out their knives and clubs, then raise billy-bob hell. No longer were men being shot on the streets of Whiskey Creek, but they were still being knifed and beaten to death. Billy knew that he would have to put a stop to that if he were to remain creditable in the eyes of the townspeople.

''Marshal Wade?'' Oliver said, not bothering to open his eyes or take his boots off the old desk that Billy had bought for him. ''I heard talk last night that Alf Tucker is still looking for someone to ambush you.''

Billy pivoted away from the window on his boot heel. ''Where did you hear that?''

''In a couple of the saloons,'' Oliver said. ''I keep my ear to the ground, and the talk is that now Alf has offered a thousand-dollar reward to the person who cashes you—no questions asked. But it's all real quiet and ain't nobody talking out loud about it.''

''I'll bet they're not,'' Billy said as he clenched his fists at his sides and then forced himself to take a seat in his office chair. He steepled his fingers and studied his new deputy, wondering if Moody could even be interested in that thousand dollars.

"Oliver, are you interested in trying to earn Mr. Tucker's big reward?"

"Hell, no!" Oliver said, a wide grin splitting his dirty face. "When we went out to the edge of town and we took target practice, I could see right away that I wasn't in your class with a six-gun. I've always just been a bounty hunter."

"You mean an ambusher and a backshooter," Billy declared, wanting to provoke his deputy to see if the man was telling the truth.

But Oliver didn't seem to mind the accusation. In fact, he said, "I never much cared whether the men I shot for their reward was facin' me, or facin' the other way. Dead is dead, right, Marshal? When a man gets killed, he don't care if he sees who puts the bullet in his gizzard."

"No," Billy said, "I suppose not. But my point is that I would imagine someone like you would think long and hard about a thousand-dollar reward."

Oliver guffawed and slapped his knee. "Now why in the world should I try to kill you, Marshal? You told me that I'd get rewarded with twenty-five percent of everything that we collect in this town. And you said I'd make about a thousand dollars a year on top of my thirty dollars town pay for as long as I care to work for you. I believed you then and I believe you now. So why in the hell would I want to ambush my golden goose?"

Billy relaxed. Oliver was deadly, but he was also transparent, and even though they hadn't really started collecting protection money yet, the ex–bounty hunter could do figures, and Oliver was just smart enough to see that being a lawman in Whiskey Creek was going to be very, very rewarding.

"So who told you about the reward?"

There was a long silence, and then Oliver said, "Pete over at the Wildcat Waterhole."

"You're sure?"

"Yep."

"And who else?"

"There's this sloppy-lookin' sonofabitch named Basil Coon. He's a drunk and blowhard and I wouldn't put much stock in what he says, but he also mentioned Alf's reward."

"I know the man," Billy said. "He's a con man and he's trying to drum up investors for some mine that he won in a poker game last week."

"He found some gold in it," Oliver said.

"He did?"

"That's right. He showed it to me and some of the other boys in the saloon. This Coon may be a faker, but I saw him collect nearly a hundred dollars and he issued some kind of stock certificates in his mine."

"Hmmm," Billy mused. "It would seem that Mr. Coon has succeeded in fleecing our citizenry. I think that, as lawmen, it is our responsibility to protect the hardworking men of Whiskey Creek from such parasites, don't you?"

Oliver grinned, and it was not pretty. "Yeah, I sure do."

Billy went over to the hat rack and collected his Stetson. "Then let's go visit Pete first, and then we'll put a stop to Mr. Coon's larceny."

"We gonna take his money?"

"I'm afraid that we might be forced to do just that," Billy said. "You see, the stocks that Mr. Coon is selling are obviously worthless."

"But them miners that bought 'em aren't going to stand still for losin' out on their investment."

"No," Billy admitted, "I'm afraid that you're right. We're going to have to return a portion of their investment."

"A portion." Oliver's eyebrows shot up. "You mean we're going to keep some of it?"

"Sure," Billy said. "Obviously, Mr. Coon will have spent most of the investors' money for his own creature comforts. All we are going to do is to recover what is left and give it back to the investors."

Billy opened the door and patted his gun. "After all, Deputy, something is better than nothing. Right?"

"Right!" Oliver said with a laugh as he patted his gun and followed Billy out the door. "But I'm glad we're going to pay a visit at the Wildcat first."

"No drinking," Billy said. "I told you that I wouldn't stand for drinking until after midnight, and then in moderation. We're going to make too many enemies to let our guards down during the next month or two."

"All right," Oliver agreed, looking greatly disappointed. "But it's going to be a trial."

"You'll be rewarded handsomely," Billy promised. "After a year or two, you'll have enough money to retire and drink all the best liquor money can buy."

They made their way over to the Wildcat Waterhole and when they entered, the saloon was fairly empty. The owner and bartender, Pete, dredged up a less-than-hearty greeting. "Morning. What can I pour you?"

"Nothing to drink for either of us," Billy said, going over to the bar and leaning forward. "Just came to see how things are these days, Pete."

Pete's eyes shifted back and forth between them as if he could read their intentions. "Business is a little slow."

"Ah, don't give me that!" Billy said. "This place is a gold mine! Why, it's packed every night, and I'll bet you must be real grateful that Deputy Moody and I have made doing business a whole lot safer in Whiskey Creek for people like yourself."

"Well, sure," Pete said, a wary look creeping into his eyes. "But there's still lots of trouble after hours. You know that as well as I do, Marshal Wade."

"Oh," Billy said with a shrug of indifference. "There's

not so much trouble. Fact is, Oliver and I have been spending extra time just to make sure that you are protected.''

The saloon owner folded his arms across his chest. ''I was able to take care of myself before you men came to town, and I'm still doing fine. What do you *really* want, Marshal?''

''Why don't we step into the back room?'' Billy suggested. ''We need just a minute to talk to you in private.''

''Uh,'' Pete hedged, suddenly looking very uneasy, ''I had better stay up here and take care of my customers. When miners are thirsty, they don't much care to wait.''

''Fuck 'em,'' Oliver hissed in a foul undertone that could be heard by Pete alone. ''Get your talky ass in the back like the marshal says before I shoot it off!''

Pete tried to bluster, but failed. He gulped and wiped his hand on a bar towel, then yelled to the customers, ''I'll be right back! Anyone needs a drink, you're going to have to wait a couple of minutes!''

The miners nodded, and then Pete went through the back door into his supply room. He turned and faced Billy and Oliver and said, ''All right, how much is this protection of yours going to cost me?''

Billy chuckled. ''I like a man that gets right to the point. Yes, sir, I do. Don't you like that too, Deputy Moody?''

''Yep,'' Oliver said, grinning wolfishly.

''All right,'' Billy continued, ''I want a hundred dollars a month paid fifty dollars every other Monday.''

''You're out of your fucking minds!'' Pete exclaimed, face turning bright red with anger.

''Deputy?''

Oliver wasn't as big or as strong as Pete, but when a six-gun materialized in his fist, Pete jumped back, throwing his hands up and pleading, ''For gawdsakes! Don't shoot me!''

''Then it'll be fifty dollars right now,'' Billy said, looking contemptuous.

''But it ain't even Monday!''

''Well,'' Billy reasoned out loud, ''no sense in us coming around day after tomorrow, is there?''

''No,'' Pete whispered, reaching into his pocket and dragging out a roll of greenbacks, ''I guess there isn't.''

''Thanks.'' Billy patted the bartender on his shoulder. ''We'll make sure that you stay well protected.''

''I thought that's what we voted you and your deputy in for at the last council meeting,'' Pete said bitterly.

''Well, I'll be damned!'' Billy cried. ''Oliver and I thought we was being hired to protect the general citizens and keep the drunks and troublemakers off the streets, not offer special protection to our town's leading businessmen.''

''I need to get back to my bar,'' Pete said, voice heavy with defeat. ''Can I go back now?''

Billy chuckled and looked very pleased with himself. ''Pete, just one more thing, then you can go back.''

''And that is?''

''Oliver tells me that Alf Tucker is offering a thousand-dollar reward for the man that drops me. I understand that you have also heard this rumor.''

Pete licked his lips. ''Well,'' he stammered, ''I did hear that, but it was probably just bullshit. I mean, there's always someone making up some rumor. I'm sure there's nothing to that reward business.''

Billy frowned. ''Well, I sure hope not,'' he said. ''Because, if anyone tries to drop me or my loyal deputy, then there will be hell to pay. You see, I'd just naturally assume that maybe you businessmen were in cahoots with Alf Tucker.''

''Not me,'' Pete said quickly.

''Good.'' Billy started for the storeroom door, and deliberately stomped his boot heel down hard on Pete's toes.

The saloon owner grunted with pain and almost reached for Billy, but Oliver's gun jumped up and punched between them.

‘‘Don’t,’’ Billy quietly advised the bartender. ‘‘Oliver and I would like nothing better than to own your saloon. Isn’t that right, Deputy?’’

‘‘Damn right!’’

Billy and Oliver walked out all smiles. When they reached the street, Oliver said, ‘‘Basil Coon is next?’’

‘‘Who else?’’ Billy asked. ‘‘We can’t have that fat bastard fleecing our citizens, now can we?’’

‘‘Nope,’’ Moody enthusiastically agreed. ‘‘We sure can’t, and I just happen to know where he’s staying.’’

‘‘Lead the way,’’ Billy ordered as he began to whistle a tune.

Chapter 17

Basil Coon was locked in his second-story hotel room counting his money and sipping a decent brand of whiskey. A cigar protruded from his porcine lips, and because the room was hot and filled with dead air, Coon was wearing only his underpants. His great gut hung like a massive sack of oats over his waist, and his face was flushed by the heat and the drink. But he was smiling as he counted the wrinkled greenback dollars.

"Six hundred and eighty-three dollars," he said, chuckling to himself. "I'll make a thousand and blow this miserable town before anyone is the wiser."

Coon leaned back and stared up at the flyspecked ceiling. His initial encounter with Whiskey Creek had started quite badly, what with being robbed by that miserable hotel clerk. Had it not been for that big bastard Marshal Custis Long, Coon knew he would have been in a real fix. But Long had restored his finances and given him enough money to began his swindle.

As soon as the United States deputy had departed to hunt down the Elko fugitives, Coon had hired an expert to salt a worthless mine. And while the job had been well done, Coon knew it was his own charm, persuasive talents, and considerable mining knowledge that had enabled him to succeed where almost anyone else would have failed. The result was a pile of cash that was growing by the hour and would, with any luck at all, top one thousand dollars by tonight.

Coon blew a smoke ring and sighed with contentment. After he reached his one-thousand-dollar goal, he would celebrate with a whore and then he'd contract a driver to carry him back to Elko under cover of darkness. Coon would much have preferred to ride the stage, but that would folly because someone would see him leaving Whiskey Creek. Coon knew that he would not have gotten five miles before his investors would have overtaken and perhaps lynched him by the side of the road.

But perhaps he should stay one more day and night and try to push his luck just a little farther. He might be able to generate a few hundred more dollars and . . .

Coon's ruminations were abruptly interrupted by the sound of a loud knock at his door. The knocking startled him badly, and he yelled, "Who is it?"

"Marshal Wade! I need to talk to you!"

"Well, Marshal, I'm a little indisposed right now. Could you come back when I'm feeling better?"

"Open the door!"

Coon scooped up his money and shoved it under his blanket. He jumped to his feet, grabbing for his pants, the hammering on his door becoming louder and more insistent. "Coming, Marshal! Just a minute, now!"

"Hurry up, damn you!"

Part of his rumpled blanket was on the floor, and Coon tripped over it and fell heavily, injuring his left knee. "Ow!" he cried.

"Open up!"

Coon half crawled to the door and unlocked it. Marshal Wade and his foul-smelling deputy shoved the door in, banging Coon hard in the ribs and causing him to cry out again.

"That hurt!"

Billy's eyes flicked over the fat man, and his mouth curled down with disgust as he closed the door behind them.

"Hey, look!" Oliver cried. "A pile of money!"

Coon gasped and saw the money that he'd tried to hide under his blanket. He belatedly realized that he'd pulled the blanket away when he'd tripped over it trying to reach the door. Despite his throbbing knee, Coon hopped to his feet and lunged for the money. Oliver got there first. He slammed Coon in the side of the face, knocking him to the floor.

"Marshal," the deputy drawled, "what do you reckon we ought to do with this cheat?"

"Collect the money as evidence."

"What evidence!" Coon squealed. "That's my investors' money! You can't take it!"

"Watch us."

Basil Coon panicked. "Marshal, if you take that money, I'll have to answer to my investors! I'll have to tell them that you and your deputy stole their hard-earned money. That'll go very hard for you."

Billy frowned. "I suppose it would at that," he admitted. "But then, it'd even go worse for you if I told your investors that you were lying. That you lost it gambling."

"Gambling!" Coon's eyes bugged. "With whom?"

"With my deputy," Billy said, glancing at Oliver. "Isn't that right?"

"That's right," Oliver said. "We had a high-stakes poker game up here last night and you lost a pile of money. Your luck was rotten."

"No one will believe that!"

"Oh, sure they will," Billy said. "We'll just hand over a little of the money back to your investors. It'll work out just fine for us."

Basil Coon drew himself up to his full height of five feet

nine and sucked in his big gut as much as possible. "I'll testify in court that you robbed me and kept part of my investors' funds."

Billy thought about that for a moment. "You'd actually do that?"

Coon wagged his double chins. "I would have no choice!"

"No," Billy said, "I suppose you would not. What a shame that would be for everyone! And just when Deputy Moody and I have about gotten this town cleaned up and law-abiding."

"Don't do this," Coon pleaded, trying to hold his pants up with one hand while he reached out in supplication with the other. "I would be happy to . . . ah, have you participate in my gold mine at a very reasonable cost."

"You would?" Billy looked surprised and pleased. "Are you saying that you would sell both of us shares at a greatly reduced price?"

"Why, sure!" Coon beamed. "I'd be more than happy to help you and your deputy that way."

"Yeah," Billy said, his smile melting into a contemptuous leer as he drew his six-gun and pointed it at the man, "I'm sure that you would."

Coon's face drained of color. He forgot about his pants, and they dropped around his ankles as he threw his hands up. "Please, Marshal, you can't just kill me. The townspeople won't stand for it."

"Maybe they would and maybe they wouldn't," Billy said. "But the thing of it is, Mr. Coon, that you are a fat, lyin', and swindlin' sonofabitch. And that's the kind of man we just can't tolerate in Whiskey Creek."

"All right! I'll go," Coon breathed. "Take the money and just let me leave quietly. All I ask for is transportation back to Elko and—"

Whatever Coon was about to add was lost because Billy stepped forward, raised his gun, and placed its barrel between Coon's eyes. The fat man jumped back into the wall and bounced a little forward. Billy shoved him back and this time, Coon struck the window. Glass shattered but, due to his huge girth, Coon would not have fallen, except that both lawmen jammed him through the window.

"No!" Coon screamed, trying to grab the windowsill and keep from falling as his pants bound his ankles and broken glass sliced into his flabby flesh. "No, please!"

It took every bit of their combined strength to push Coon the rest of the way out the window, and he screamed all the way down, the sound ending very abruptly when he struck the alley.

Billy and Oliver gazed down at the bloated, bloody figure lying still in the alley.

Billy said, "What do you think?"

"I think he's probably dead."

"But we can't be sure. Better make sure."

"How am I supposed to do that?" Moody asked.

"He's lying on a pile of broken glass, isn't he?"

The deputy blinked as he understood Billy's intentions. "You're right," he said, his voice lacking its usual mockery. "I guess he probably landed right on top of glass and maybe a splinter of it cut his throat."

"Seems entirely likely," Billy said, nodding his head. "Now go on before someone gets to him first. I'll take care of the money."

"Twenty-five percent, right?"

"That's right."

Deputy Moody turned at the door. "There's at least five hundred dollars that I can see. Probably more."

"We'll have to give some back or we'll have a hell of a time with the miners."

"I guess so," Oliver said. "How much?"

"We can decide that later," Billy replied. "When you've finished our work."

Oliver nodded and hurried outside while Billy collected

and counted the money. He smiled and folded the thick wad of bills, then crammed them into his pocket.

As he left the room. Billy begin to whistle a tune. And why not? Being the marshal of Whiskey Creek was getting to be mighty lucrative, thanks to that fool United States Deputy Marshal Custis Long.

Chapter 18

Longarm hadn't bothered to search for the wounded mustang killer named Ralph. No doubt the man had slithered off into the sagebrush and somehow managed to escape. Longarm was quite confident that Ralph would never return to northern Nevada to kill mustangs again.

Now, Longarm was pushing hard to get his sole prisoner, Phil Pate, back to Whiskey Creek, where he would pick up Donita York. Unless she had changed her mind, they would both take the stage to Elko, where Longarm would deliver the bank robber to the local authorities.

As they neared Whiskey Creek, Pate said, "I got a lot of friends in this town, Marshal."

"Is that a warning or a promise?"

Pete's wrists were bound and his ankles were lashed to his stirrups. "Marshal Long, you can take it any damned way that you want."

"Well," Longarm said, "I'm not a bit worried about your friends. The thing that has me most concerned is the fate of the new deputy I hired. He's quick with a gun and plenty brave, but I'm afraid he might not measure up to taming that town."

"Measure up, hell!" Pate said with derision. "Ain't nobody ever going to tame Whiskey Creek. Why, didn't you ever hear what happened to the last couple of marshals that tried to lay down the law?''

''Yeah,'' Longarm said, thinking of what he'd heard about Donita's murdered husband. ''But I just had a feeling about this Billy Wade and—''

''Billy Wade?'' Pate's jaw dropped and he stared. ''Did you say Billy Wade?''

''Sure. Do you know him?''

''No, but I've heard a hell of a lot about him.''

''That's not surprising,'' Longarm said. ''Billy was a pretty fair deputy marshal in Abilene, Kansas, and down in Santa Fe, New Mexico.''

''That's right,'' Pate said, ''and he was damn near lynched in both them places.''

It was Longarm's turn to gape with surprise. ''What are you taking about?''

''Billy Wade is a smooth-talking gunfighter that puts fear into everyone he meets,'' Pate said. ''I heard about what he did in Tucson about two years ago. He shot down the local marshal and two of his deputies, then tried to buffalo the whole damned town. He would have too, if it hadn't been that the citizens banded together and drove Wade and his friends out.''

Longarm shook his head. ''We can't be talking about the same man. The man I deputized is too young to have done all the things you're telling me. Why, *this* Billy Wade can't be more than twenty-five years old.''

''He's older than that by at least five years because, down in the Texas Panhandle country, they say that Billy Wade killed four Comancheros and then shot up a cantina full of Mexican bandits. I heard it was a bloodbath.''

Pate grinned, liking the confusion and disbelief he was seeing on Longarm's face. ''Yep, if you deputized Billy Wade, you just sort of opened the henhouse door and let in the fox among the chickens.''

Longarm scoffed. ''We're talking about Whiskey Creek!

Not some dainty and genteel little town with mostly church-going citizens. Nobody is going to tame Whiskey Creek by themselves. They might calm it down a little and establish a measure of law and order, but that's about the limit.''

''I'll tell you this much, Marshal Long, if you hired the same Billy Wade that I've heard about, you hired a man that is pure poison. And what's he up against in Whiskey Creek anyway? Just a bunch of damned miners.''

''They're a tough crowd.''

''Sure! They get liquored up and then they're first-rate at busting heads. But they're not gunfighters. Billy Wade will kill a few and then he'll figure out a way to take control of that town.''

''You're crazy,'' Longarm said, realizing that he did not sound very convincing.

''No,'' Pate said, ''*you're* crazy! I don't know what you're going to find when we get to Whiskey Creek, but it damn sure won't be what you expect. And while I never met Billy, I was a friend of his late cousin, Ezekial, and maybe he'll take that into account after he guns you down.''

Longarm looked away with a scowl. He didn't want to believe any of what he was hearing, but there was enough that sounded legitimate that he was damned glad to be forewarned. Longarm just hoped that Pate had the wrong man.

It was nearly sundown when Longarm rode into Whiskey Creek, and since he was passing Donita's house and a light was shining through her window, Longarm thought it might be worth a minute to stop and say hello. Not only did he want to see Donita's lovely face and figure again, he wanted to find out if there was any truth in Phil Pate's dire predictions.

''What the hell are we stopping here for?'' Pate bitterly complained. ''Gawddammit, I'm sore and tired. I want to get to jail and see your face when you learn that Billy Wade has taken over this whole damned town.''

''Keep still,'' Longarm ordered, climbing wearily down from his horse and tying both the roan and Pate's horse to Donita's fence. ''If you try to escape, I swear I'll shoot you out of the saddle.''

''There's no need for me to escape,'' Pate said, forcing a tired grin. ''Billy will help me out.''

Longarm started to say something, then changed his mind. He had ridden so many miles in the last week that his legs felt like wooden stumps. He was bone tired, and even if Donita had greeted him stark naked, he wouldn't have been able to rise to the occasion. There were times, Longarm realized, when a man's body was simply too exhausted to meet the challenge of his fertile and foolish mind.

''Don't move,'' Longarm ordered from Donita's porch.

''No need to, Marshal Long,'' Pate called. ''But what are you going to do, get a little stinkpot from that woman on her front porch swing?''

Longarm turned. ''Mind your mouth!''

Pate laughed, and Donita came to the door. ''Who is it?''

''It's me, Custis,'' Longarm announced, breaking into a big smile.

Donita let out a small cry of joy and flung the door open. She jumped into his arms, and her lips were sweet and her kiss passionate.

''Come on inside!'' she begged, trying to drag him through the door.

''I . . . can't just yet,'' Longarm said, digging in his heels.

''Woo-wee!'' Pate exclaimed. ''No wonder you was in such a big damned hurry to get back here!''

Donita ducked under Longarm's arm and stared at the man on horseback. ''Who is that?''

"My prisoner. I had to shoot the other two and a couple of their friends. But this one got lucky."

Donita moved back around to gaze up at him. "What are you going to do with him?"

"Take him to the jail for safekeeping and then—"

"No, no!" she pleaded. "You don't know what's happened here since you left."

"Why don't you tell me?"

"Can you come inside?"

"Not without bringing in the prisoner and I'd rather not do that," Longarm said. Donita looked beautiful, and the scent of her perfume was driving all thoughts of sleep from his brain.

"Just tell me what is wrong," he said.

"It's Billy Wade," she began, "the man you hired to watch over Ike Moffitt. He's awful, Custis! He even tried to . . ."

Donita began to shake uncontrollably, and Longarm led her over to the porch swing.

"What are you waiting for, Marshal, jump her!" Pate crowed. "Now that you got her where you want her, do it!"

"Shut up!" Longarm hollered before he knelt before the upset young woman. Gently taking her hands, he said, "What did Billy Wade try to do?"

"He came here right after you left. He was in my bedroom and he would have . . ." Donita gripped his arm. "He's evil, Custis! I had a pistol or he would have taken advantage of me. As it is, he's been killing people, and he's even managed to get his own city council elected."

"And the townspeople just took it?"

"He's hired a deputy. A man named Oliver Moody. He's almost as bad as Billy, and they've got this town scared half to death. Mr. Tucker and Mr. Judson tried to oppose Marshal Wade, but they just vanished."

Longarm had been in town just long enough to know that Alf Tucker was the most powerful and influential man in Whiskey Creek and that Henry Judson was his best friend and almost as wealthy and respected.

"They vanished?"

"Yes!"

Donita took a deep, steadying breath. "Just last night. The bank didn't open this morning, and no one has seen either Tucker or Judson all day. Everyone in town says that they both must be dead. Why else would Alf Tucker not open his bank?"

"I don't know," Longarm admitted. "I'm still having trouble believing everything that I've heard."

"You had just better believe it," Donita warned. "In fact, the best thing that we could do is just to ride on out of Whiskey Creek with your prisoner. Custis, we could reach Elko and then—"

"No," Longarm decided. "I can't just run away from a disaster that I created. I selected Billy Wade. I knew he was arrogant and cocky, but I never thought he was a killer or that he'd take over Whiskey Creek. I was more worried that I'd return to find him ambushed like your late husband."

"My husband was a brave man, but he was naive and trusted too many people," Donita said, tears filling her eyes. "But Billy Wade and his deputy are wolves in sheep's skin. They're using their badges to throttle the life out of this town. They're utterly ruthless."

Longarm stood up, his mind churning as he tried to fathom how he could have misread Billy so badly.

"What are you going to do?" she asked.

Longarm heaved a deep sigh. "I need to get some sleep and have a little time to think clearly."

"You can stay here, of course, but . . ."

Longarm knew that Donita was thinking about his prisoner. "Don't worry about him," he said, wheeling around and leaving the porch.

He untied Pate's feet from the stirrups and dragged him from his saddle.

"Hey, what are you going to do with me! What—"

Longarm was out of sorts and out of patience. The man's crude remarks of a few moments earlier still burned, and so Longarm drew his six-gun and pistol-whipped Pate hard enough to put the bank robber to sleep well into tomorrow morning.

"My God, did you kill him?" Donita asked as Longarm dragged the unconscious man into her parlor.

"No," Longarm said, dropping Pate and retying his feet, then rolling him over on his belly and cinching up his hands and feet so that Pate was hogtied.

"Do you have a dishrag or bandanna? Something that I can stuff into his foul mouth just in case he wakes up in the night or starts howling?"

"Yes, but won't he choke?"

"Only if I get lucky."

When the outlaw was taken care of, Longarm hurried back out to the street, brought their horses around behind the house, and put them into Donita's corral where they would not attract any attention. He unsaddled both animals and made sure that they had feed and water, then staggered into Donita's house and collapsed into a chair.

"You're exhausted," she said.

"Yeah," he admitted, "I am. I need some sleep. I'll get up at dawn and make my move before the marshal or his deputy are fully awake."

"What do you mean, make your move?"

"I mean that I intend to arrest Billy Wade and Oliver Moody."

"But they're the law!"

"Well," Longarm hedged, "so am I. I put your late husband's badge in Billy's hand, and now it's my job to get it back—one way or another.''

"Come on and lie down,'' Donita said, pulling him up from the couch and leading him into her bedroom. "Lie down and I'll pull off your boots and get you ready for sleep.''

"Thanks,'' Longarm said, his eyelids so heavy that they felt as if they were sheets of lead. "Thanks.''

"What time do you need to wake up?''

"I need to be out of here just before dawn. Where do Billy and his deputy sleep?''

"I think Moody sleeps at the jail. I hear that Billy is living with a woman that Alf Tucker was fond of seeing. Her name is Rose.''

"Where?''

"The big two-storied hotel.''

"All right,'' Longarm sighed. "Good night.''

Donita bent and kissed his mouth. "Are you still going to take me to Denver with you?''

"If you still want to go.''

"Of course I do!''

"What about this house and all this nice furniture? You can't just walk away from it.''

"I sold this house. There's even a man who offered me two hundred dollars for the furniture.''

"Take it,'' Longarm said with a yawn, "and we'll leave after I settle with Wade and Moody tomorrow.''

Her fingers traced lightly across his lips. "I wish you would change your mind.''

"I can't,'' Longarm whispered as she turned out the bedside lamp. "I have to make things right.''

"No,'' she breathed, unbuttoning his shirt and slipping her cool hand inside to rub his flat belly. "That's not what I meant.''

Longarm felt a stir of arousal. "In the shape that I'm in, I just wouldn't be much good to you, honey.''

"Let me be the one to decide about that," she said. "And I promise, this won't take but a few minutes."

Longarm summoned up a weak grin as Donita began to unbuckle his belt. He knew that he should have protested, but now his body seemed to be telling him otherwise.

Chapter 19

''Did your husband have a shotgun?'' he whispered, leaning over Donita's bed and kissing her cheek.

''Yes.''

''Where is it?''

Donita rolled off the bed. ''How do you feel?''

''Rested,'' he lied.

''Are you sure?''

''Yeah. Where's the shotgun? It's starting to get light outside and I need to get the jump on that pair.''

Donita padded past him, hips swaying in the lamplight. Longarm followed her out of the room and into her late husband's little office.

''Here,'' she said, dragging a double-barreled shotgun out of a closet.

''Shells?''

''Yes.'' She found them in a desk drawer. ''Here. What should I do while you're gone?''

''Start packing your personal belongings. Have you got a neighbor friend?''

''Sure, Mrs. Hudson, but . . .''

''Make a list of the things that you want forwarded to Denver and I'll pay the stage line when we board for Elko,'' Longarm instructed.

"Are we really leaving today?"

"That's the plan," he said, hoping that it would all come to pass.

Longarm quickly inspected Phil Pate. The man was still out cold. "If he wakes up before I come back and he tries anything, just club him with a rolling pin or something and put him right back to sleep."

"I can do that."

"Good," Longarm replied, taking the young widow into his arms and squeezing her tightly. "And don't worry. This is going to turn out just fine."

"After I make the list, I'm going to start praying."

"That would be fine too," he said, loading the shotgun and heading outside to see the first light of the sun fire the eastern horizon.

Whiskey Creek was a ghost town at this hour, and Longarm moved quickly up the street. It took him less than five minutes to reach the jail, and when he tried the knob, he was not surprised that the door was locked.

Longarm wiped his face and scowled. He thought a minute, and then he affected a slur to his voice and began to pound on the door. "Marshal? Marshal, I need help!"

There was no response inside, so Longarm pounded the door even harder. "Marshal! I said I need your help!"

Finally, a sleepy voice called, "Go away or I'll kill you, you drunken bastard!"

"I'll pay you to help! I got money! Open up, Marshal!"

Longarm heard bedsprings creak in protest, and then he heard the deputy pad across the floor, muttering and cursing. When the door opened up, the butt of Longarm's shotgun connected solidly with Oliver Moody's jaw. The man crashed over backward and tried to get up, but Longarm was on him like a cougar on a calf. He whipped a thundering uppercut to Moody's face and laid the deputy out stone cold.

Longarm set his shotgun aside and dragged Moody over

to the jail cell. It took him a minute to find the keys, and then he put Moody inside, locked the cell, and shoved the key into his pocket.

"One down, one to go," he said to himself as he headed out the door.

The hotel where Billy Wade was staying with Rose didn't even have a name. It was just called The Hotel because it was by far the biggest and the best in Whiskey Creek. Longarm passed across the lobby and hammered on the registration desk. When no one responded, Longarm climbed heavily up the stairs and tried the first door.

After he knocked for several minutes, a sleepy voice called, "Who is it?"

"It's the marshal! Which room is Rose in?"

"Two-oh-five, dammit!"

"Thanks."

Longarm walked up to Rose's door and tried the knob, knowing that the door would be locked. He stepped back and unleashed a load from the shotgun that ripped the knob and the door apart. He kicked open the door and jumped inside.

Billy Wade was reaching for the holstered pistol that was hanging on the headboard.

"Freeze!" Longarm shouted.

But Billy's hand was already on the butt of his gun, and it was coming out of its holster faster than an eye could blink. Longarm knew that he was a dead man if he hesitated for even a moment. So he pulled the second trigger of the shotgun and a roar filled the room. Billy's arm disappeared, and so did half of his face.

"No!" Rose screamed. "Billy!"

Longarm lowered the empty shotgun and walked over to the dead man. It wasn't a pretty sight, and he was glad that the room was still quite dim.

"What did he do with Tucker and Judson?" Longarm asked.

"You sonofabitch, you just killed him!"

"Did he kill Alf Tucker and Henry Judson?"

Rose shook her head and tears began to spill down her cheeks. Like Billy, she was stark naked, but Longarm scarcely noticed. He did notice Billy's coat and the shiny badge that gleamed in the faint shaft of early morning sunlight.

Longarm took the badge and slipped it into his pocket, knowing that it was something that Donita would want to keep.

"Sorry about the mess," Longarm said. "And I sure wish you'd tell me what happened to Tucker and Judson."

"They're in Hell!" Rose screeched. "Just like you'll be for killing my Billy!"

"I might go to Hell," Longarm admitted, "but not for killing the likes of Billy Wade."

Longarm backed out of the room because he feared Rose wouldn't hesitate to kill him, given the slightest opportunity. He trod down the hallway and then down the stairs to the lobby, where a staring hotel clerk, still wearing his pajamas, now stood.

"Do you know if the stage for Elko leaves today?" Longarm asked.

"Huh?"

"The stage. Does it leave today?"

The clerk nodded and stammered, "Leaves in about three hours."

"Good," Longarm said, shuffling wearily out the door. "Then at least three of us will be on it."

Watch for

LONGARM AND THE BRANDED BEAUTY

233rd novel in the exciting LONGARM series
from Jove

Coming in May!